CW00847045

THE AUTHOR

BILLY BOB BUTTONS is the multi-award winning author of thirteen children's books including the Rubery Book Award FINALIST, Felicity Brady and the Wizard's Bookshop, the much loved The Gullfoss Legends, TOR Assassin Hunter, TOR Wolf Rising, the Cool Kids Book Prize WINNER, Wide Awake, the hysterical Muffin Monster and the UK People's Book Prize WINNER, I Think I Murdered Miss.

He is also a PATRON OF READING.

Born in the Viking city of York, he and his wife, Therese, a true Swedish girl from the IKEA county of Småland, now live in Stockholm and London. Their twin girls, Rebecca and Beatrix, and little boy, Albert, inspire Billy Bob every day to pick up a pen and work on his books.

When not writing, he enjoys tennis and playing 'MONSTER!' with his three children.

BILLY BOB BUTTONS' BOOKS

FELICITY BRADY AND THE
WIZARD'S BOOKSHOP

THE GULLFOSS LEGENDS

TOR
ASSASSIN HUNTER

TOR
WOLF RISING

TIFFANY SPARROW
SPOOK SLAYER

I THINK I MURDERED MISS

DROWNING FISH

MUFFIN MONSTER

THE BOY WHO PIDDLED IN HIS
GRANDAD'S SLIPPERS

THE HUNGRY GRASSHOPPER

WIDE AWAKE!

the
TOR
TRILOGY

TOR WOLF RISING
is the second book in
THE TOR TRILOGY,
the turbulent story of a Swedish mercenary
infested by the spirit of Skufsi Tennur,
the most sinister, most unholy werewolf
of the Hamrammr tribe.

THE WISHING SHELF PRESS

ISBN 978-1537776897

Published by THE WISHING SHELF PRESS, UK.
www.bbbuttons.co.uk
Printed by Amazon.
Edited by Alison Emery, Therese Råsbäck and
Svante Jurnell.
Cover by Laura Tolton, www.laurajanetolton.wordpress.com.

TOR
WOLF RISING

by

Billy Bob Buttons

HUNT THE SWORDS TO WIN

Within the text of TOR Wolf Rising you will find a number of hidden swords. Over every sword there is a word and the words form a complex riddle. If you can solve the riddle, and the riddle in TOR Assassin Hunter and TOR Mutiny's Claw, you can win a wonderful prize: a ruby in a tiny silver chest.

For Mary and Eve

'It is a man's own mind, not his enemy's, who tempts him to evil ways.'
Buddha 624 BC

'Evil needs only a timid victim.'
Ayn Rand (writer) 1905-1982

.

TOR

WOLF RISING

Or

The Further Ramblings of a Swedish Botanist

Tuesday, 3rd October, 1871
128 Days to Assassination Day

1330 hours, The Flying Spur, just off North Africa

I scowl so hard, my eyebrows almost meet the stubbly whiskers on my chin. Clomping footsteps echo over me, dust showering my curls and upturned cheeks. Then they slowly ebb to a tiny patter. Three men, possibly four, difficult to tell, up on the deck by the stern.

Unfortunately for me, I'm down in the galley in the bow, but the words, 'HANDS UP DOGS OR WE KILL YOU!' still rock the cups on the shelf and the four rusty dessert spoons in the cutlery drawer.

The Flying Spur, a fifty year old clipper, is a very small ship.

Typical! The crew is under attack by bandits and I'm trapped in the kitchen. No sword. No musket. No boots. Just straw sandals on my feet and a ridiculous and, even if I do say so myself, very tasty pot of fish stew clutched menacingly in my hands. And to add insult to injury, I'm dressed in violet polkerdot shorts that Compass Cob, the ship's navigator, lent me and a rosy-pink apron with a yellow duck embroidered on the front pocket.

The thump of feet! The pong of - I sniff - yes, feet, smelly feet. But not up on the deck. Closer. Much closer. Hastily, I drop the pot on the hob and snatch up a wooden spoon.

The door rebounds off the wall and a bald, bullish-looking man storms in, 'MAD' tattooed on his right cheek, 'KILLER' tattooed on his left. Yellowy scabs swarm over his puffed up face and he has way too many chins to count. I suspect he's not here to sample my stew. Or maybe he is!

'WHERE'S ALL YOUR CARGO?' the brute bellows, brandishing a very rusty, crooked-tipped sword. His sunken eyes look wild and hungry for trouble.

I shrug. 'I'm just the ship's cook,' I inform him sourly. I decide not to tell him I'm on the run from a gang of assassins for destroying their plan to murder the King of Sweden. 'The skipper never even bothered to tell me we had company for supper,' I rattle on. 'Typical of the man. Never thinks of his crew.' I drop chopped carrots in the pot. 'Fish stew,' I tell him before I dip the wooden spoon in it and put it to my lips. 'Hmm. Needs pepper. A lot of pepper.' I look crossly to the pirate. 'PEPPER!' I cry.

Scratching his shiny skull, the bandit turns to the spice shelf. 'Pepper,' he says softly. 'Is it yellow or...?'

I wallop him with the pot and he drops to the floor in a puddle of cod eyes, fins and perfectly chopped carrots.

'Yellow pepper!' I roll my eyes. The culinary skills of a street rat.

After apologising profusely to the pot of fish

stew for ever doubting it, I creep to the back of the Flying Spur, pull on my boots, snatch up my trusty rifle and hook my sword on my apron string. I decide to keep the apron on. Well, you never know, perhaps the ship's visitors worship birds. The hawk, perhaps, or the mystical phoenix. My eyes drop sceptically to the yellow duck stitched to the pocket. Hmm, maybe not.

Gingerly, I climb half way up the stern ladder and peer over the lip of the hatch.

I spot three bandits up on the deck by the ship's wheel. Probably Spanish, judging by the accents, two of them the size of rhinoceros with droopy bottoms and wobbly walrus jowls; belted shorts peek out from under waterfalls of fat and grubby torn vests ride up to their armpits. The third is lollipop-skinny with bushy Neanderthal eyebrows, a whiskery chin and three wispy curls clinging stubbornly to his well-polished skull. He is dressed a little better in a tatty tunic and a lumpy pelican-pink cravat, his crimson velvet pantaloons tucked in his boots. I see there is a belt riding his hips but it is so colossally fat it almost seems to cut him in half. He is yelling orders to his chums and must be the boss.

Thankfully, I see no muskets, only swords. Very old swords by the look of it; sort of chunky with cloth-wrapped hilts and tapered tips.

I spy the Flying Spur's crew too: Commander Church, Compass Cob and the boy, Oddjob, trussed up like fowl and roped tightly to a barrel of rum. My feet curl up on the rung of the ladder. No help to be had there then.

Anxiously, I watch the skinny pirate hook Church's chin in his fingers. 'El gringo I just sent below had better find a chest of silver in y' ship's hold,' he snarls. His English, I note, is pretty good for a Spanish bandit.

'There's not even a copper penny in the ship's hold,' the Flying Spur's skipper shoots back bravely.

Good for him, I think.

The crook's nostrils twitch. He then rewards the skipper's boldness with a punch in the belly and a spit in the eye. 'We will soon see, y' old fool. Anyway, it's not important. This ship is the perfect prize. We will sell it in Egypt for ten camels and a well in the Sahara.' He smirks and

turns his pitiless eyes to his fellow bandits. 'Toss 'em in the Med, boys. Let the sharks enjoy a tasty supper.'

A cold chill floods my body and I suck in my cheeks. I must act, and I must act NOW! But I need a plan. A Wellington at Waterloo sort of plan. I know. WING IT! Perfect.

I clamber lithely up the top three rungs of the ladder and level my rifle on the belly buttons of the three Spaniards. 'Drop your swords,' I cry in my very deepest tenor, 'or I'll, er, drop you.' Hmm, not very original, but hey, I'm only the ship's cook; and I am in a duck apron.

Wide-eyed and droopy-jawed, they turn to look at me. Water laps on the hull, a bird in the crow's nest squawks, then two of the chunky, Sinbad-style swords drop meekly to the deck.

I risk a cocky wink to the ship's crew. 'I'm not just a whiz in the kitchen,' I cheerily tell them.

Skipper Church rolls his eyes. I suspect my smug wit is lost on him.

The skinny pirate, however, keeps his wits and his sword and turns a pitying eye on the musket clutched in my ivory-knuckled fists.

'Pretty apron,' he remarks. 'Very slimming.'

'You can borrow it,' I shoot back flippantly. 'Match your pink cravat.'

'Hmm. Funny man.' He scowls at his bandit crew and rubs his bristly chin. 'Pick up y' swords, y' bunch of jellyfish,' he lazily scolds them.

Sheepishly, they do so.

Then he puffs up his chicken chest and turns back to me. 'Listen up, Duck Boy. There be,' he counts bandits, 'one, two, three of us and just, well, how can I put it, a ninny in a yellow apron. Do the maths and YOU drop it.' His eyes narrow to tiny evil slits. 'We can do it my way or the 'broken jaw' way. Personally, I prefer the latter of the two; so much fun to watch.'

Squaring my shoulders, I stubbornly thumb back the hammer of my musket. After ten days cramped up on a ship the size of a bathtub, I'm sort of in the mood for a punch up.

With a wolfish smirk, the skinny brigand brings up his blade. 'A broken jaw it is then. GET HIM BOYS!'

With swords in fists and banshee yells, they stomp over to me. But I can spot no subtlety to the attack, no trickery, and I can hardly miss. I

pull the trigger, reluctantly - well, sword vs musket is hardly sporting - but to my dismay there is not so much a 'BOOM!', but a lazy sizzle and a yellowish bloom of smoke.

My father always told me, 'Son, keep your sword razor-sharp and your gunpowder stone-dry.'

'Nuts,' I murmur, the only word for it. I must remember to listen better to my elders.

'Run for it!' yells Church.

But where to? I'm on a hundred foot ship. Now, if he'd yelled, 'Swim for it!'. Oh well, in for a penny...

I drop the musket and hastily pull my sword from my apron. My wonderful 'wing it' plan is not so wonderful now, but Tyrfing's cold steel in my fist floods my stomach with fire and I charge recklessly in.

Our swords do a speedy tango. Three on one. NOT GOOD! But, oddly, my enemy seems slow to me, clockwork toys, the springs old and badly worn.

I know I will win.

Two swords fly up, the first bayoneting the mast, the second the barrel of rum, a foot or so from Compass Cob's left cheek.

He throws me a squinty-eyed look.

'SORRY!' I holler.

My boot ricochets off a shin, my elbow batters a jaw. Teeth splinter. A howl and two of them drop to whimpering, curled-up balls.

Wow! This is fun.

Now only the skinny pirate is left on his feet but I see blossoming terror in his eyes. He storms over to me, half tripping over a mop and a bucket of dirty deckwater. Thankfully, his swordsmanship seems to be on par with his clumsy feet and I effortlessly parry his attack, the steel tip of my blade nipping his knuckle.

With a yelp, he drops his sword.

But the plucky bandit's not thrown in the towel yet and he plummets to his knee after it. Suddenly, from nowhere, a volcano of fury erupts in me and I see red. Mercilessly, I skewer his foot to the deck. The result is a yell so shrill, the birds in the crow's nest fly off in panic.

Well, the powder in my musket may not be dry, but I can still tell my father I keep my sword pretty sharp.

Coldly, I listen to my victim blubber and cry. His helplessness almost seems to feed my wrath and I long to bury my sword in his chest, see

his blood on my...

'*Yes, yeeeessss, he's scum.*' The words echo in my mind. '*Do it. Do it now. BE A MAN! FINISH HIM!*'

For a second, I'm tempted, my fist cemented to Tyrfing's hilt. Then I blink and slowly my shoulders droop. I may be a mercenary, but I'm no cold-blooded murderer.

In my four years of fighting other mens' wars I have never enjoyed bloodshed. Even shooting Gripenstedt's son, my sister's killer, sickened me to my stomach. So why, I wonder, do I now enjoy battering jaws and splintering teeth. Why I am so tempted to skewer this man to the jib-boom?

Confident there is no fight left in them, in any of them, I recover my sword from the bandit's foot and hook it back on my apron. I say 'my sword' but did I just control it, I ponder, or did it just control me.

I mull this over for a moment, idly thumbing the ruby encrusted in Tyrfing's golden hilt. Was it the sword that spoke to me; tempting me to murder a man on his knees? I chew on my lip, tasting blood. Is there a demon in this shiny hammered steel?

I'm pulled from such alarming thoughts by a yell from the skipper. 'Sorry to disturb you, Tor...'

'Oh yes, sorry.'

Quickly, I undo the knots tying the Flying Spur's crew to the barrel. Then I march back over to the three bandits sprawled like starfish on the ship's deck.

'Help me to lock 'em in the hold,' I order Compass Cob.

I'm not his boss but the old man nods anyway and grimly, he yanks the bandit's sword from the barrel of rum.

Then I look to the boy, Oddjob. 'Go fetch rum and we'll dab it on this crook's foot. The alcohol will stop gangrene setting in.'

'No way!' carps the bandit. 'That'll ruddy hurt, that will.'

'OK,' I relent. 'It's your foot. I know, we'll let it fester for a few days, you know, till it's all mushy and smelly. Then we can saw it off.' With a wicked grin, I turn to Compass Cob. 'Is there a saw anywhere on the ship?'

'Nope, but I got a blunt chisel,' he offers helpfully.

'Excellent! We can chisel it off. Yes, a much

better plan.'

This seems to put a stop to the bandit's whining.

'Oddjob.' I wink to the boy. 'Go fetch the rum.'

'No, Tor. This is my ship.' The skipper's lips twist up and he smirks cruelly. Then, mirroring the crook's words, he flippantly orders his crew, 'Toss the sorry lot of them in the Med.'

There is a snivelling cry and the skinny pirate clambers to his knees, clawing at my leg like a hungry dog.

I scowl, my fists on my hips. Bandits or not, we cannot just throw them to the sharks. It seems my sense of chivalry has returned and I'm very thankful for it. I see the rest of the crew look equally upset by the skipper's ruthless plan.

Church beckons me over to the ship's wheel. Knowing I must try to stop him, I kick the weeping pirate off my foot and, with Cob and the boy standing guard over the bandits, I walk dutifully over.

'I don't think the crew's too happy to just throw them in the...'

But the skipper interrupts me. 'I'm only

joking,' he whispers. 'I spotted them on a raft just off Lisbon and I thought they'd been shipwrecked. Then, when I stopped to help them, they put a sword to my belly. I ruddy peed myself; drenched my trousers and filled my boots. So I just thought I'd frighten the bejeepers out of them too.'

I grin and I feel my spirits lift. I'm happy I was there to put a spanner in the Spanish crooks' plan for the ship and her crew, but I'm nobody's executioner. I swallow, the fury I'd just felt still simmering like hot oil under my skin. I hope not, anyway.

I shoot a look over my shoulder at the cowering bandits. Even from here I can smell them, a potent mix of old dirt and snivelling spinelessness. 'I think it did the trick,' I tell him dryly.

Thoughtfully, the skipper rubs his stubbly chin. 'We will sink the vermin's raft, patch them up and drop them in Gibraltar. The British own it. It will be a hangman's rope for them there.' He shrugs. 'But better than sharks' teeth.' Then his eyes widen and a playful sneer curls his upper lip. 'I wonder if there'll be a reward. Gold or, well, a bottle of rum will do.'

'You conned me,' protests the bandits' boss. 'You told me you had no cargo, but if there's nothing in your hold, why's there a mercenary on y' ship?'

'Mercenary?' titters the skipper. The rest of the crew chuckle too and I just try to look innocent. The apron helps. 'I can only presume you're referring to the Flying Spur's cook.' He slaps me in a brotherly sort of way on the shoulder.

'COOK!' a second bandit scoffs him, spitting a tooth on the deck. 'No way! If he's a cook, I'm a monkey's uncle.'

Skipper Church shoots me a cheery wink. 'If you doubt my words, Pirate, then I strongly recommend you try Chef Tor's plum crumble. Very tasty.'

'IT IS! IT IS!' chorus Oddjob and Compass Cob, grinning manically.

But I'm too lost in thought and do not catch the crew's complimentary words. There's a pool of blood on the deck; I always throw up when I see or smell blood, so why, I wonder, am I not throwing up in the very handy bucket of dirty deckwater.

Thursday, 5th October 1871

Dear Mother,

I'm sorry it took me so long to put pen to paper but 1871 has been truly challenging. In France I lost many of my men to the German cannons and I just spent a very difficult year in London trying to find the murderer of a child I met in Stockholm.

It is a long and complicated story but on the welcome day Gripenstedt is taken by the devil, I will be on the next ship to Jokkmokk and I will then tell you it over a tall glass of lingonberry and a tasty Fah Sang Pehng bun.

I did not succeed in England, the murderess cleverly evading me. So, with low spirits and a bitter anger gnawing at my stomach, I now find myself on a ship heading for China.

I do not know my exact plans but I hope to travel up to Beijing and see the splendour of the Forbidden City and I will try my utmost to visit Grandmother in Ningpo. I remember you told me her village is south of Shanghai but how far south, I do not know.

The ship I'm on is aptly called the Flying Spur. Tell Father she's a 100 foot clipper with 3 tall masts, hammocks for 4 and a top speed of 18 knots. She's old but sturdy and has the playful spirit of a wild cat, battling her way through storms with courage and finesse.

The crew of three, for the most part, is jolly and interestingly eccentric:

There's Commander Church; he's the skipper. He's Danish, a lazy fellow with the belly of a pregnant whale and the aroma of a wild pig. I long to throw him in the water to wash off the stink. But he's cheerful and funny and he enjoys losing to me at chess, a worthy quality in any man.

The navigator is called Cob but everybody calls him Compass Cob. He's a pipe smoking Scott who tells me he's not set foot on land for over 50 years. He knows everything there is to know about ships and fishing and he's schooling me in the tricky art of tying a Dropper Loop knot.

Finally, there's a weedy lad by the name of Oddjob. He's from Norway. Oslo, I think. He's only 13 and

he never says a word. Not to me anyway. Cob told me he lost his family to yellow fever so his uncle, the skipper, took him on. His job is to swab the deck, peel the carrots and empty the loo - a rusty bucket with a lid. It must be a pretty dull life, but he always seems to go about his work with a whistle on his lips and a skip in his step.

You'll be surprised to know - and Father will laugh hysterically - I am, in fact, the ship's cook. A day or so ago, I hit a pirate with a pot of fish stew so now the crew call me Tinpot Tor.

The ship's kitchen is tiny, the size of the hen hut Father and I built, and my tools consist of a wooden spoon, two rusty pots and a frying pan. Unfortunately, the spoon has not got a handle and the frying pan has 20 years of fat welded to it. I cook a lot of beef Wellington and cod stew - my gravy is still a bit lumpy - and the crew insists on potato with everything: chops with a dollop of mash, chicken on a bed of mash and rhubarb smothered in mash. And there must always be coffee on the hob, Skipper's orders.

We left Copenhagen two weeks ago and Compass

Cob told me we will be in Malta in two days. So far, it has been a wonderful trip and now I hardly ever throw up, even when the storm hit us in the English Channel.

We stopped off in Portugal and Gibraltar to pick up chickens and rum and I spotted a number of very unusual flowers. I'm keeping a record of all the plants I see on my travels in a book. I will keep it for you and if I can find Grandmother, I will show it to her too. I know she is a keen gardener.

In six days we will be in Egypt, the mystical land of the sphinx and the pyramids, and then we will be travelling south on the Suez Canal. I'm very excited to see this engineering marvel. It only opened in 1869, so Cob told me, and it is the major artery for ships carrying cargo from China and Japan to the bustling ports of England. Crews no longer need trek all the way around Africa and the treacherous Cape of Good Hope.

I'm enjoying this journey very much. I know Father loved his old ship and I think I now know why. In England I was becoming obsessed by 'tomorrows'.

But here, on the Flying Spur, I can only think of 'todays'.

I must stop there for I'm needed in the kitchen. The coffee pot is almost empty and I'm cooking swordfish for dinner. Compass Cob hooked it yesterday off Majorca. A 4 footer. He tells me the flesh is softer than butter.

We shall see.

Your loving son,

Tinpot Tor

Wednesday, 11th October 1871

Dear Mother

Our stop in the port of Gozo in Malta was very interesting. It is a tiny island of lush palm trees, sand and wooden huts just south of Sicily and yet to be embraced by the modern world. We took on food there, mostly melons, apricots and bananas, the skipper bartering for them with tobacco and a barrel of rum.

We left Malta after only a few hours and sailed for Egypt and the Suez Canal. Unfortunately, the weather has not been kind and the poor Flying Spur has had to battle through almost three days of brutal storms. It was very difficult to cook and at night I regularly fell from my wildly swinging hammock, thumping to the deck with the prowess of a sack of spuds.

The sun blessed us with her return only yesterday and I cooked the hungry men a plum crumble to celebrate. There is a new member to our crew. A dolphin! She enjoys playing by the bow of our ship and is a wonder to watch. Oh, to be so free.

This morning we finally got to the Suez Canal.

There, with the sun climbing up over the desert, we were anchored to a motor barge. We must be towed through the canal as the wind is predominantly westerly and the canal runs north to south. The skipper thinks the Flying Spur is almost obsolete, soon to be replaced by steam ships and propellers. I hope his prophecy is mistaken. Billowing smoke is far less romantic than billowing sail.

I sit now on the bow of the ship watching the deserts of Egypt pass me by. It seems to be a very empty land. No animals, no flowers, only the odd cactus braving the shimmering midday sun.

The canal, I must say, is not very wide and we had to stop in a lake to allow traffic to pass by. According to Compass Cob, our ship's encyclopaedia, the canal is owned by the Suez Canal Authority under the Arabic Republic of Egypt. It is 164 kms long, 26 feet deep and took 10 years to dig. At a ponderous 8 knots, it will take us almost 16 hours to travel the length of it.

Soon we will be in the port of Aden, a British owned town just south of the Canal in the country of Yemen. There we will stop for fresh water and to stretch our legs. Then, on Sunday, we begin the next leg of our journey. We must cross the vast Indian Ocean to Sri Lanka.

It is very hot here and no matter where I try to hide, the sun seems to find me. Even in the cabin I feel as if I'm wrapped in fur. I know it is freezing up in Jokkmokk in October but, to tell the truth, I sort of miss it. Even the snow!

All my love,

Tor

PS
Compass Cob was correct. Swordfish is softer than butter.

Monday 23rd October, 1871

Dear Mother,

Today you find me in tropical Sri Lanka. The island is only small, perhaps twice the size of Lake Vänern, and if you look on a map you will find it just off the bottom of India.

The journey from the port of Aden in Yemen to here was awash with incidents.

It took almost eleven days and for the most of it I saw no land and no sister ships. It was like being in a desert but considerably wetter.

The first five days were a breeze. Literally! The wind was strong and westerly and Cob hooked a small tiger shark which I cooked for three suppers in a row. The crew and I enjoyed it; it reminded me of tuna, and chicken – tunery chicken, but the flesh was salty and a little dry and my teeth had to battle to chew through it.

Then, on day six, the wind suddenly dropped to a whisper and the Flying Spur's sails went limp. The skipper reckoned a big storm was on the way, so to pass the time until it hit us, we all went swimming in the ocean. All but Compass Cob who, it seems, after 50 odd years on a ship still can't swim. I offered to teach him but he told me, very sternly, if God had intended him to swim he'd have given him gills and fins. An interesting argument. Anyway, I'm glad to say even the skipper went for a dip and he smells much better for it.

Then the most amazing thing happened. I spotted a whale. A sperm whale according to Cob. In truth, a sleeping blind man would have spotted it; it was bigger than our barn and swam all the way up to me. For just a second my fingers brushed barnacle-encrusted skin then it slipped to the depths with the grace of a lazy hawk.

Then, on day six, just as the skipper had predicted, the storm fell on us. I lashed myself to the mast in the bow and watched. It was terribly frightening but amazing too. The sky was blacker than the pits of Kiruna and the sea churned and bubbled with the ferocity of a wild bull. That day I truly saw the power of the hand of God.

Unfortunately, a gust of wind snapped the aft mast in two and when the storm finally passed we had to limp our way to Sri Lanka at half speed.

The skipper reckons we will be in port until Friday. By then the mast will be fixed. He told me to relax and see a little of the island until then. So I'm now in Chilawa, a tiny hamlet just north of the capital city, Colombo. I'm sitting on a cliff under the shade of a lemon tree watching the water and a shoal of jumping fish and trying to draw.

Little Sylva has been very much on my mind on this trip. I see her eyes everywhere. Jade green and full of fun. I wish she had been there to swim with the whale and to sit here with me now and laugh at the jumping fish. I miss my sister terribly, Mother. I miss every freckle on her chin. And her laugh. I so miss her wonderful laugh. I know shooting Gripenstedt's son took me away from you and Father, but I shall never regret what I did. To this day, I hope the murderer rots in hell.

Our next port of call will be the British colony of Singapore. Then the Flying Spur will push north.

past the islands of Borneo and Taiwan and up the coast of China. Compass Cob expects us to be in Shanghai in two weeks.

Thinking of you.

Tor

Thursday 10th November, 1871

Dear Mother,

Two days out from Shanghai and a nervous snake sits in my stomach. The Flying Spur has whisked me 4,000 miles from Copenhagen and my many problems, but I wonder what new problems I must not face here in China.

It took us three weeks, not the two weeks Compass Cob predicted, to sail from Sri Lanka to here. We stopped to stock up on food in Singapore but under the insistent eyes of the port master there we also took on cargo. Cannon balls, swords and muskets for the Chinese army. It seems China is having a spot of trouble with rebels and a new attack on them is planned. It took us two days to stow the cargo and with so much ballast, the ship can now only muster a miserly 9 knots, half her usual speed.

Over on our port side, a stone throw away, is China. It looks very green and lush, the clumps of trees speckled with wooden huts and tiny pig farms. Every minute or so we pass a fisherman, his nets spread from the back of his boat like the fan of a peacock's tail.

Travelling north from Sri Lanka, the weather has turned much colder. The wind is damp and a fat belly of cloud shadows the sun.

The boy, Oddjob, is now talking to me a little. I think my squid hotpot loosened his tongue. It seems Compass Cob is his hero, he had a cow but lost her in a poker game and his gut instinct still tells him the world must be flat.

My next letter will be from Shanghai. Finally!

Your loving son,

Tor

PS
You remember when I was six and I fell in the well at the bottom of the garden and, after that, how claustrophobic I was. Well, the crew's cabin is tiny but it never seems to bother me. I must be cured.

Saturday, 12th November, 1871

Dear Mother,

My first day in Shanghai has been truly amazing. The Flying Spur docked here yesterday night at 11 o'clock and this morning, I borrowed a tatty town map from the skipper and set off to explore.

I spent the morning seeing the sights in a taxi. Basically, a man pulling a trap. He must be so fit! Then I went to the Yu Yuan Gardens. Truly magnificent. There is a wonderful rockery there and a 50 foot tall sculpture constructed of hundreds and hundreds of yellow rocks.

I must say I feel very tall here and it is very difficult to blend in. Everybody, but for me, is barefooted, and everybody, but for me, has on a grey tunic and a fur-lined cap. I put on my cavalry uniform and sword; you never know, I might meet the empress.

China is not just a different land to Sweden, it is a different planet. Everybody in the city seems to be in a hurry and they remind me of scurrying mice. I think I must buy a bicycle. Perhaps then I will fit in better. Men sit on the streets playing cards and market stalls sell cobs of corn and rice from rusty bathtubs. Turn a corner and I never know who, or what I will happen upon. A camel perhaps or a pig. Or maybe a crazy old granny cycling full pelt.

If you wish to go to the loo here, it seems you just bob down and go in the street. It is disgusting. Consequently, the town is filled with many interesting aromas; it is so bad, the skipper, in comparison, now reminds me of a sweet smelling rose. I'm sincerely happy I'm not barefooted too, for who knows what I will step in next.

The Flying Spur will stay in Shanghai harbour for only three days. Then she will set her compass for England with her hold overflowing with tea. But I will stay here. I will travel the country and fill my little book with exotic flowers. Perhaps if I fill my mind with petals, stems and roots I can smother the memory of Gurli, the murdered child in Stockholm. I can but hope.

But my sister I can never forget.

I'm now sitting in a café just by the Pudong River, enjoying a cob of corn and a tiny, tiny cup of liquorice-black coffee. I can see the post office from here and I plan to go there soon to post all of my letters from my trip to China. Then I'm off to the Flying Spur for a good night's sleep.

Tomorrow is a new day.

I love you,

Tor

Sunday, 13th November, 1871
87 Days to Assassination Day

0312 hours, Shanghai Docks

Hunkered down by a pile of crab baskets, the ninja, swathed in black, instantly spots the wharf sentry. He is slumped on a stool by the door to his hut, his eyes hidden in Shen Bao, the town's newspaper. His interest in sports will be his undoing, the ninja thinks ruthlessly, putting a blowpipe to his lips. He blows sharply and a split second later a dart is embedded in the sentry's artery. The poor man slumps to the floor.

Keeping to the shadows, the ninja sprints by the splayed body and over to where the Flying Spur is anchored for the night. The ship is almost twenty feet from the dock but he jumps it effortlessly.

He drops to his knees, his jackal eyes hooded and wary of danger.

A bell tolls dutifully in the bay and the bow of a whaler knocks the dock with the persistency of a rent collector. But there's no billowing cry, no yell for help.

The ninja peeps in the cabin window to see Major Tor and the rest of the crew asleep in hammocks. The major, he sees, is in his cavalry uniform, his sword on his belt. Hopping up on the cabin roof, he pulls a tiny mechanical drill, a bottle and a ball of cotton from his pocket. Slowly, he twists the drill and burrows a hole in the wooden roof sprinkling sawdust on the major's eyebrows. Then he burrows a second hole. A spy hole. He puts his eye to it. Perfect. He drops the tip of the cotton through the other hole and slowly unwinds it till he sees the tip of the cotton is only a whisker from the snoring major's lips.

Now for the tricky job.

He pops the cork on the bottle and drips a tiny drop of venom down the cotton.

Drip.

Drip.

Drip.

His hand tremors just a little and it drips on Tor's bristly chin.

The ninja sucks in his cheeks, but he keeps his wits. Jiggling the cotton in his fingers, the next drop lands perfectly on the major's top lip.

He licks it away and flips over on his belly.

Success!

Secreting his ninja tools, he jumps off the roof and skulks down the steps to the cabin. The door, he finds, is not locked. His spy in the crew has performed his duty well.

He creeps by the snoring crew and stops by the major's hammock. Spotting a book clutched in Tor's hand, he snaps it up, slipping it into a hidden pocket. Perhaps it will be of interest; help him to know this westerner, this enemy of SWARM. It might even help him to find the major's flaws.

With the fluidity of a farmer snatching up a sack of corn, he flips the sleeping trooper over his shoulder. There is not even a flutter of the major's wood-flecked eyelids. The henbane sap did the trick.

Church, the Flying Spur's skipper, grunts in his sleep and in a flash, the ninja is by his hammock, the tip of his sword pressed to the top button of his mucky, coffee-splotched shirt. But thankfully, for Church anyway, he sleeps on.

On the pads of his split toe boot, the wily kidnapper creeps back up the steps to the deck. There, he stops, puts two fingers to his lips and

chirrups, perfectly imitating the shrill of the yellow-billed loom, a bird common to Shanghai harbour.

His cold black eyes rest on a bank of swirling fog just off the port bow. The major on his shoulder is bulky and uncomfortable but it is no problem for the ninja. He is the very best of the best. He frowns and balls up his fists. But for the telltale tremor of his fingers.

Suddenly, the brutish bow of a colossal iron ship rips a hole in the mist, her two funnels billowing smoke. She draws parallel to the Flying Spur and the kidnapper coolly steps from the wooden deck over to the iron-plated one.

There he hands his sleeping prisoner to a lanky man with carroty-red curls.

His job is over. For now anyway.

Thursday, 17th November, 1871
83 Days to Assassination Day

1730 hours, Hornet Temple, Ningpo

The room I'm in is the size of a landowner's

barn. The floor I see is wicker, the walls thin and papery-looking and on a low bench in the corner there sits a bunch of spiked iron balls and curve-bladed swords. Over by the wall, under a tapestry showing hundreds of men scaling the walls of a castle, I spot what looks to be a dressmaker's dummy but in place of feet it has tiny yellow wheels.

I'm stood rather precariously on the shiny, extremely slippery lid of a beer barrel, my hands knotted in rope all the way up to my elbows and a noose lovingly caressing my neck. I'm no Alfred Nobel, but even I can tell I'm up the creek without a paddle. In fact, I'm not even in the canoe.

I'm happy to see I'm still in my cavalry uniform anyway. Mind you, I'm minus my most important tool, my sword, and I wonder, idly, if Prince Frederick's ring is still hidden in my tunic pocket.

There is a 'foot on wood' rasp and my eyes cut to a screen door over on the far wall of the room. With my cowardly knees knocking up a drum roll, I watch it slither slowly open.

To my astonishment, the lanky man I spotted six weeks ago on Copenhagen docks

lumbers in. He has hands the size of shovels, ruddy blotchy cheeks, piggy eyes and a shocking crown of carroty-red curls. He instantly reminds me of a circus clown but without the flippery feet or the twirly bow tie. There is, I see, a sort of sulky, sullen look to him; a boy who lost his toy car to the school bully. I sniff. Even from here I can smell him. He stinks of old smelly boots.

A second man follows him in. He looks Chinese and is much shorter, with a stern crew cut and the beefy shoulders of a smithy. There is a black splodge on his cheek, a birthmark perhaps, and it puts me in mind of a cloud-shaped ink blob. He walks on the pads of his feet, a panther on the hunt, his short legs swirling up his black robe and the sword on his belt.

The clownish-looking brute stays over by the wall but the oriental man struts over to me, stopping only three feet short of my barrel. He plants his feet so firmly on the floor I doubt even a herd of elephants could uproot him.

'Good evening, Major Tor, I'm Sensei Wu Tong,' his English is almost perfect with just the hint of a drunkenly slur, 'and I'm the

master of Hornet Temple, this, er, ninja school.'
He flaps a lazy hand. 'And this is the Rimankya
Room.'

Drowsily, I look to his devil-black eyes and
shiver, a chill creeping up from my boots to my
belly. He has the eyes of a butcher.

'You probably still feel a little woozy. But
don't worry, it'll pass. The sleeping tonic I
brewed for you was not very powerful, just a
drop of henbane and a hefty lump of cow dung.
Incidentally,' he bobs a finger at me, 'henbane is
a very good truth serum so I'd er, watch my
words if I were you.'

I nod stupidly, my thoughts fuzzy, my skull
full of cotton wool. In a dizzy spin of fantasy, I
wonder when Church and his crew will storm
the room and rescue me.

'I know no Swedish whatsoever, but my
English is good, yes? I went to Oxford; I was a
student in philosophy there. By the way, I'm
from Japan, not China, a small town by the
name of Tokushima on the island of Shikoku. It
seems, Major Tor, you and I are a long way
from home...'

The clown grunts; a bullish snort.

'But I'm rambling; I do apologize.' He nods

to his buddy. 'Mr Bee over there travelled all the way from London to tell me our employer, SWARM, is a tiny bit upset with you; the fly in the jam, so to speak, and they want me to swot you.'

'Ointment,' I correct him, his bullying words sharpening my dulled mind. 'The fly in the ointment, and don't bother to dress it up. I get it. You plan to kill me.'

He seems to mull this over for a moment, then his thin coppery lips twist up. 'Perhaps.' He snaps his fingers and the clown throws him a sword. My sword.

'A pretty toy, Major,' he murmurs, studying it, 'but still just a toy. Hardly the tool of a professional ninja.'

'I'm no ninja,' I snap back. 'I'm an army officer, and my sword is not a toy. Not in my hands.'

Wu's perfectly trimmed eyebrows climb his brow. 'We shall see,' he says.

His wrist snaps and a silvery object cuts my noose. I jump nimbly to the floor.

'Clever trick,' I murmur.

'A throwing star,' he schools me. 'Shuriken in Japanese.'

Warily, I watch him march up to me. He pulls his sword; so fast I hardly see it. It plummets and the rope binding my hands thumps to the floor.

Then he throws me my sword.

'The work of the ninja assassin is honourable, Major,' he slips the clown a wink, 'and profitable too.'

'There is nothing honourable in murder,' I spit, remembering poor Gurli.

The tips of our swords meet and he is on me. He is brutal, his blade a blur and I step hastily back, tumbling over the barrel.

Gentlemanly, he steps off, allowing me to find my feet, and over by the wall Bee trumpets his approval of my clumsy footwork and poor swordsmanship.

I feel a fool; a silly schoolboy in a classroom full of scholars.

'A ninja is a master of jutsu,' Wu tells me. 'Kenjutsu, the sword; kyujutsu, the bow; yarijutsu, the spear and bojutsu, the stick. He can climb a cliff, jump a river and escape a prison in seconds. He is the perfect assassin.'

'Just kill him,' sneers Bee, his words low and gravelly. 'He'll never be a ninja. He's just

fodder for the cannons.'

A tornado of fury swells up in my body; the fury I felt when I had battled the pirate on the Flying Spur.

It's him...

Or me.

He attacks but I shoulder him off me, twirl my wrist and thrust. Our swords spark and just for a split second I see a way in. But with Tyrfing's cold steel tickling the whiskers on Wu's chin, I stop. '*Not now.*' A soft whisper from nowhere. '*We need him.*' The anger I felt is abruptly washed away, as if a bucket of icy water has been thrown over me.

To my horror, I suddenly feel the cold steel of my enemy's blade under my own chin.

Slowly, I lower my sword.

'You remind me of a doddery old woman with a broom,' Wu mocks me. He too lowers his sword. But I think he knows I had him. I can tell by the arch of his eyebrows, the stony set of his jaw. Oh yes, he knows. 'But there is a hunger in you, Major, I can see it.' He shoots me the jackal's eye. 'Skill too, I see. But you must not allow your feelings to choose the target for your blade.'

Swiftly, he drops low, his foot sweeping me off my feet and I cartwheel to the floor. Desperately, I lift my sword but it is torn from my hand.

He drops to a knee and eyes me keenly. Stubbornly, I return his look. 'Join SWARM, Major, and you too can be a ninja assassin, respected by your peers and the object of terror to your betters.' I feel the tip of his blade tickling my cheek. 'Or you can say your prayers and I can put you in your tomb. Choose.'

I swallow. I detest SWARM with all of my being. They murdered Gurli and with this in mind I do choose.

I choose...

1900 hours

I expected a cold damp cell in a spidery cellar but I get a cosy room on the top floor of Hornet Temple. The floor is carpeted in bamboo, there is a tiny window with a potted orchid on the sill and a crackling log fire is doing a wonderful job of chasing away the seeping damp.

In fact the only way I know it's a cell is the

fact the door's locked.

A dish of beef and rice sits by my sleeping mat, proof they intend to feed me, and next to it rests my sword. My new tutor, Wu, had handed it back to me and sent me off, Bee in tow, to rest for tomorrow.

For tomorrow I begin ninja school.

Part of me, however reluctantly, had been impressed, even amazed by the speed of this Wu-fellow, and the opportunity to be schooled in the art of the ninja is just too tempting to say no to.

He had been remarkably swift with his sword and normally I'd be overjoyed just to paper cut his thumb. But now, it seems, I'm not such a 'normal' fellow and when we had crossed swords today, I know I had had him. Just for a split second, when the acid had bubbled in my blood, my blade only a whisker from his chin. Only the whisper had stopped me from killing him. But the whisper of whom, I wonder.

It is very uncharacteristic of me. I'm a musketeer, not a swordsman, and I'm usually clumsy to boot, but with Tyrfing in my fist I feel almost invincible.

But it is not just the sword.

On my journey to China, I had watched myself transform. Suddenly, I could chop carrots blindfolded and pick up the anchor with my baby finger. After six weeks on a cramped ship I should be weedy and wobbly on my feet, but I'm not and I don't know why.

But I do know I had held purposefully back today. I had not shown Wu or this Bee-character my new powers. I wish for them to think I possess the fighting skills of an arthritic pig farmer. Then, when I do strike...

Also, if I'm honest, I'm a little frightened by my sudden potency, this acid in my blood. I wonder what it is and why is it in me. I wonder, if soon, when the blood flows, will I listen to this angel. Will she still sway my sword?

I hold my hands over the fire but I find no comfort there. In fact, the sizzling red embers bother me and I worry a spark will land on my new ninja robe.

I tramp over to my tiny window well away from the spitting logs. My cavalry uniform is on my sleeping mat. Astonishingly, the ring had still been in my tunic pocket and now it is hidden in the heel of my boot.

The sun is beginning to set, a lazy blob on the horizon, but oddly I can still see the temple's trimmed lawns and a stone dragon crouched in a pond, belching water. I even spot a Chinese cracker flower, not ten feet from the pond.

I remember from my Grandmother Toyi's letters how mystical Chinese gardens can be. Every flower, no matter how tiny, is a symbol. The flowering plum, I know, represents the power of will and bamboo is a symbol for strength. The banana tree is chosen simply for the soothing way the bananas knock in the wind. A Chinese garden is almost poetry, a haven for the thinker and a shelter from hardships.

The temple, I see, is on a low hill encircled by rows upon rows of lush green crops. Mostly hemp and cotton by the look of it, the fluffy cotton reminding me of tiny lumps of snow. Not too far away in amongst a thicket of cypress trees, I spot a cluster of red-slated roofs. A village, and help, perhaps, if I need it.

I wonder how far I am from the port of Shanghai. The journey here is a drowsy haze. I remember being on water and the gentle rock of a ship and my shoulder still throbs from being tossed on a wagon. But had I travelled for a day, a week or even a month?

But now I'm here, I must admit I'm intrigued and I wonder what Wu has in mind for me. But whatever he's planning, there's no way I will ever work for SWARM. But I will let Wu tutor me and then I will turn on him and SWARM and destroy them with the very skills he schools me in. This is the perfect opportunity to infiltrate this toxic club of ninja and destroy it from within.

I often try to picture Gurli, her cherry-red curls, hazel eyes and petal-blossoming smile. Sadly, she is a little hazy now, but I remember Alfred Nobel had been her hero and her only wish had been to be an inventor and help the world. Soon this web of assassins will pay for murdering her.

With this in mind, I hunt out a stub of pencil from my tunic pocket. Then I pick up my book and begin to sketch the orchid on my window sill.

Ninja School, Day 1
82 Days to Assassination Day

0135 hours

My mind will not let me sleep.

I tumble over and over on my futon, my sheets twisted and knotted, drenched from my twisting body.

I see a cavern floor strewn with skulls. Then, just for a second, a mammoth tower of water erupting up from a snowy valley. Icy brooks, rocky cliffs, a waterfall thundering into a canyon. All jumbled up. Like me, they tumble over and over...

Suddenly, they stop, and on my futon in Hornet Temple, I lay completely still.

There is a low chanting and slowly I look over my furry shoulder. In my tortured mind, I spot a tunnel. It is blacker than the night between the stars but I can still see it perfectly: the low roof, the glistening icy walls. I feel my nose twitch. I know this tunnel. It is the tunnel I saw when Skufsi Tennur bit me.

Slowly, I trot up it. Skulls blanket the floor and not wishing to step on them I keep my eyes to my feet. No, not feet. Paws! White paws peppered black.

I get to a corner. The chanting is much louder here but the words echo off the walls and I cannot decipher them.

I know, I must get closer.

I know, only then will I understand.

o6io hours, Hornet Temple

'This, Major Tor, is the ninja short bow.' Wu holds it up for me to examine. 'It is only three feet tip to toe but with it you can hit the thorn of a rose at a hundred and fifty feet, a squirrel at three hundred.'

I don't shoot flowers, I want to tell him, and squirrels hardly ever attack me, but I hold my cheeky tongue and, thoughtfully, finger the bow. Three hundred feet; not too shabby, but I still prefer a bullet. Unfortunately, my rifle, along with my box of inks, is back on the Flying Spur, unless the skipper swapped it for a bottle of rum.

'Whale bone,' he incorrectly answers my frown, 'in three segments so it can be

dismantled and hidden in a pocket.'

I remember what he had called my sword and I copy him. 'A handy toy,' I mutter depreciatingly.

No doubt noting my tone, he looks to me and hooks his eyebrow. 'Very.'

'Sorry,' I say, my hands up in mock surrender. 'It just seems a little, you know, old school for a SWARM assassin.'

Wu responds with a depreciating tut. 'The quiver, or rimenkya in Japanese, can hold up to twelve arrows,' he ploughs on, 'and slips tidily over the shoulder.' He shows me.

My new keeper, Bee, had woken me to a chilly dawn with a vigorous kick of his boot. I did not sleep well, my mind full of creepy tunnels and ivory skulls. So, still rubbing my eyes, I had been led out to the lawns.

There, in the shadow of Hornet Temple, I had been met by Wu, and with the yellow clouds curdling and thinning and with the sun peeking cheekily over the hills, my schooling in archery, kyajutsu in Japanese, had begun.

I peer over at the temple. The walls tower over me and look almost unclimbable and the door looks to be two feet thick. The roof is no better. It is covered in red tile and drops steeply to a curly, flipped-up rim. The rim, I see, is crowned with barbed wire.

It is a fortress, I think dejectedly.

Our only company seems to be the birds in the trees and the hum of insects, so I ask Wu if I'm his only student.

'Yes, it is autumn in China now. The ryu, school you call it, is shut until December.'

'So you opened your doors just for me,' I chide him. 'I'm honoured.'

'Don't be.' His lips hint of a smile. 'SWARM pays me well to babysit the enemy.'

So, I'm still 'the enemy'. Reluctantly, I return to the archery lesson. A hundred whys, whos, wheres and whens twirl in my mind but I dare not push my luck. 'It's a well-crafted tool,' I admit, 'but I much prefer the accuracy of the rifle...'

In a flash, he slips an arrow from the quiver, swiftly fits it to the string of the bow and lets it fly. A rosy red plum on a far off tree thumps to the lawn, effectively ending my protests.

'Hand cannons, muskets you call them, were actually invented here, in China in the 13th century.' I can see Wu is mentally patting

himself on the back. 'If I remember my history, they were employed in the battle of Ain Jalut in 1260. I'm sorry to burst your bubble, Major,' I can tell he's not, 'but the West did not discover them for another two hundred years.'

This is news to me.

'Do not be fooled by the simplicity of the bow. Ninja prefer it to the rifle. You see, it's a lot, lot better. Here, you try.' He steps up to me and with a tiny encouraging nod, offers me the bow and the quiver of arrows.

My nostrils twitch; he reeks of apple cider. This man's a drinker. I wonder idly how old he is. Forty? Fifty? Difficult to tell. There is a patch of grey in his left eyebrow but not even a tiny wrinkle on his bronzed skin.

With a cynical frown, I take the bow and arrows. I can feel Bee's critical eyes on me; no doubt he's hoping I will miss.

I put on a show of clumsily trying to fit the butt of the bamboo arrow to the string, but Wu stops me.

'Remember, a ninja is an assassin, not a brave cavalry major,' he says with a splinter of spite. 'He must always be ready to flee the coop. So, bend your back knee.' He shows me and begrudgingly I mirror him. 'Good. Now, if necessary, you can push off your back foot and run for the hills.'

I nod. This is sort of fun so I decide to show off.

With the string well past my cheekbone and the arrow level with my eye, I target the plum tree and shoot, but the arrow ricochets off a banana tree almost a hundred feet short.

A little crestfallen, I lower the bow. It seems my newly-discovered powers do not extend to archery.

The clownish Bee snorts and begins to slow clap but a withering look from Wu quickly stops him. So Wu's the boss of this sweet little coupling. Interesting.

'Major, the bow is very different to the rifle. The bullet is direct, the arrow is not. You must remember to allow for the curve of the arrow's path.'

I nod curtly. I feel foolish and I wonder why I want to impress this man so much. He is my enemy, after all.

'For every 1,000 arrows you shoot, you will improve by 1 percent. Only 99,999 to go, Major Tor.' He bows. 'Keep up the good work. I will

return soon.'

He pads off and I'm left under the watchful eye of Bee.

~

I spend the rest of the day working on my archery skills, stopping only for a pithy lunch: a bowl of beef and rice, my second in two days, and a cup of lemony spring water. It is surprisingly hot in the November sun, the blustery wind doing a miserable job of chilling the droplets on my brow. Nevertheless, Bee's sentry duty is unwavering; a pit bull watching over a rabbit hole.

By sunset there is a nasty welt on my finger but I'm happy to see twenty or so plums littering the lawn.

My teacher, Wu, walks back over. He looks to my chaffed hand and the nest of plums and nods. 'Bravo, Major. I'm happy to see there will be plum crumble for supper. In fact, you can bake it for us. I happen to know how much you enjoy juggling pots and pans in the kitchen.'

Scowling, I watch him pull a book from his pocket. Who, I wonder, had told him I liked to cook.

'I did so enjoy your sketchings, Major.' Wu looks to my keeper. 'It seems, Mr Bee, my ninja student here is the budding botanist.'

But the clown just laughs mockingly; probably the only laugh left in him and rolls his eyes in disgust.

'The lemon trees of Sri Lanka were particularly fascinating,' he persists, handing me back my drawings. 'You see, Major, I too enjoy a spot of botany, but of a very different kind.'

So, Wu not only kidnapped me, he snatched my book too.

My eyes narrow but I swallow my bitter words with a Cheshire cat grin and retort, 'A plant is innocent, just a child. It's only thirst is for water and sun.'

Wu claps his hands gleefully. 'A poet too. Marvellous! But sadly, incorrect. The plant is hardly innocent. Here, let me show you.'

He twists sharply on his heel and strolls off, but not back to the temple. I suspect he expects me to follow him, so I do, my shadow, Bee, doggedly on my heels

It is, I must admit, very pretty here. Over a

dozen richly tinted flower beds litter the trimmed lawn, and in a corner, by a stone sundial, a yellow rose cheekily climbs the trunk of the banana tree my errant arrow had hit. We amble by nests of soft-tongued orchids, lofty bamboo trees and hundreds and hundreds of blossoming chrysanthemums.

But many of the flowers I simply do not know; unusual for me, and my fingers itch to sketch them.

'Major, did you know, and not many do, there must be well over two hundred different plants that can kill? Two hundred! Amazing, I know. You might find the venom in the petals, the stems, the tubers, the roots, or even the bark. Why, in these very flower beds you will discover the sweet perfume of the hemlock, the deceptively pretty petals of the monkshood and, look, over there, the red berry of the cuckoo-pint. Very nasty customers and, trust me, not so innocent. But such plants can be effective tools in the hands of the ninja.'

'A coward's way to kill,' I murmur, remembering the impostor who had played the role of Duke Solbakken so well and had put blowfish blood in the king's punchbowl.

'Major, Major, SWARM did not invent the clever ploy of murdering the enemy in his bed. The Thugs of Kali did in the 8th century followed by Hassan of Iraq and his fanatics in the 11th. You see, the assassin is part of our history, our world culture.'

Twaddle, I think, my temper spiking, but I keep my lips tightly shut.

We stroll by the tree I spent the day attacking and I scoop a plum up off the grass. It is shiny and plump but when I chew on it the yellow flesh is surprisingly bitter.

'In Italy in the 16th century,' Wu persists, 'a lady, Madonna Teofania di Adamo, discovered the cure to the problem of 'annoying husbands'. She actually sold her 'medicine' in shops.' He barks a laugh. 'The result, six hundred fewer husbands and six hundred happy widows in the world.'

We stop by the pond and I look casually down the hill to the nest of roofs I had seen from my bedroom window.

'Ningpo,' Wu tells me flatly.

Choking on my foul-tasting plum, I try to look indifferent to this astonishing bit of news. Grandmother Toyi's village!

'Jump it, Major.'

Momentarily lost for words, I spit pulped plum on a firecracker bush. 'Ningpo?' I finally muster.

'NO!' he trumpets, grinding his heel in the grass. 'The pond. Jump it.'

I look to the muddy pool, my eyes narrowing. 'You must be joking,' I protest. 'It's over twenty feet.'

'Firstly, I never joke,' he tells me stiffly, 'and, secondly, you think too much. Whether it is possible or not is not important. Think only, I must jump this pond, I will jump this pond. Only then will you succeed.'

Mumbling profanities, I back up three steps.

'Oh, and Major, try not to land on any of my golden dart frogs. The skin, you see, is full of venom; a drop of it will kill a rhino.'

Wonderful! 'How sweet of you to worry,' I mutter bitterly.

'Oh, I do,' he smirks, 'but for the frogs, not for you.'

Clenching my teeth, I sprint for the bank. I jump, pulling my knees up to my chin. Nine feet, ten feet...

I hit the water with a tremendous splash.

I look up to see Wu, the ghost of a smile on his lips. His chum, however, is bent over, hooting and cackling so much I wonder if, perhaps, he is having an asthma attack.

'Admittedly, it is important to know the skills of pond jumping before attempting the actual pond jump,' murmurs Wu matter-of-factly. 'I must remember to demonstrate them to you tomorrow.' He pulls a hip flask from the pocket of his robe and drinks from it. Then he twists on his sandaled heels and, whistling a cheery tune, he strolls off. 'Keep up, Major, plum crumble for supper.'

It seems, I ponder, up to my knees in slimy pond weed and lily pads, that Wu enjoys a good joke after all.

My nostrils twitch and I smell my armpits. And why is it I smell so much of wet dog?

Ninja School, Day 2
81 Days to Assassination Day

0610 hours

'Today is Unarmed Combat Day.' Rubbing

his hands, Wu shows me an alarming number of ivory teeth. 'We will begin with togadure-ryu.'

Bee titters; a bad omen.

Instinctively, I clench my jaw. My second day of ninja school and I'm back in the temple, in the Rimankya Room. I slept deeply and I had not been happy to feel the clown's boot at five thirty in the morning. No doubt my body's still recovering from yesterday's lessons, though, astonishingly, the welt on my finger vanished overnight.

Wu steps up to me. No matter how much he hurts me, I must not show him the true extent of my own fighting skills. It is important he and his chum think I'm a bumbling fool.

'The most important weapon in the ninja's bag of tricks is not the sword, the blowpipe or the bow. It is the element of surprise.' Only a foot in front of Wu, I nod warily. Whatever togadure-ryu is, it's going to hurt.

Suddenly, his hands fly up and he claps me hard on the ears.

Bells ring and I cry out in agony. With a whimper, I drop to my knees.

'So you see, Major Tor,' I can tell he is

shouting but I only just catch his words, 'this particular method of disabling the enemy can be very successful.'

'No,' I mumble scornfully. 'Honestly?' My skull feels as if it's been split open with a blunt hatchet.

Bobbing down in front of me, he pats my shoulder. 'I, of course, only hit you very, very gently.'

With a pathetic, almost babyish whimper, I topple over, thudding to the floor. I roll up in a ball.

'A cup of kumis, Mr Bee,' Wu hops to his feet, 'till the major recovers. Then, when he feels up to it, I will hit him a little harder.'

0720 hours

'This here is Hattori.' Wu wheels over the wooden dummy from the corner of the room. I must say it looks very human: quartz-rock eyes, mopish curls, even a bristly moustache and a mole on the cheek. 'Named after the legendary ninja, Hattori Hanzo,' Wu tells me, 'of the 17th century.'

I nod. I remember it from the other day, when I had stood on the beer barrel with the noose around my neck. Such a sweet memory.

'Today we will be working with the fist, the foot and the knee. Let's begin with the fist.' He looks over to my keeper. 'Mr Bee, if you will kindly demonstrate for the major here.'

His elephant-footed chum plods over and without a moment's thought, thumps the mannequin. My chin drops to my collar bone and wide-eyed, I study what's left of poor Hattori's ribs.

'Gotta hurt,' I mumble.

'Tremendous job, Mr Bee.' Smirking, the clown swells up his sparrow chest and lumbers off back to his sentry post by the door. Then Wu looks to me. 'He's very talented.'

'Hmm,' I nod mockingly, 'for a Neanderthal.'

His jaw hardens and I spot the tiny, almost imperceptible twitch of his left cheek, but he lets it go. 'Now then, Major Tor, your turn. Hattori's torso is a little er, destroyed, so hit him on the chin. Hard.'

Gritting my teeth, I curl up my hand and thump it, almost shattering my knuckle. With lewd words spurting from my lips, I nurse my fingers in my armpit.

'No, Major,' he barks, a dangerous spark in his eye. 'He's your enemy, not your sixty-three year old mother. I told you to hit him hard. HARD!'

He knows my mother is sixty-three!

My eye sparks too but I need him to think I'm trying. I swallow my rebellious thoughts and dutifully I follow his order.

Wu rolls his eyes and tuts. 'No, no, NO! You must pretend Hattori here is trying to murder you; not just you, your family too,' his eyes narrow evilly, 'even your poor sister, Sylva. Such a tragedy.'

My top lip flips up in a snarl. He knows way too much. WAY TOO MUCH! And I very much want to wipe the sneer off his face

'*Do not be foolish,*' says the whisper. '*He will help us to destroy him.*'

Destroy who, I wonder. Spider? But the words still my temper. I keep my wits and with a blood-curdling growl I turn on the dummy.

'Now hit him hard,' Wu instructs me. 'Pretend he's Gripenstedt's son.'

THUD! THUD! THUD! THUD! THUD!

'Good, Major. Good. You will be a ninja in

no time.' He bows. 'I will pop back soon to check on your progress.'

Two agonisingly long hours later, he dutifully returns, but by then my fist is a blood-spattered pulp and my mood is volcanic.

He looks to the dummy and his eyes narrow. 'Excellent,' he murmurs. 'Excellent! I see Hattori's chin is very slightly dented.'

I roll my eyes. I very much doubt it is. The dummy's chin is rock hard and all I can see is my blood all over it.

'Look!' Wu knocks on the wood with his knuckle. 'I think you even splintered it.'

'Yes, well, I pretended he was you,' I say jokingly. Well, sort of jokingly.

He titters but I spot his hand shift a little closer to the sword on his belt. 'Whatever works for you, Major. Now, rest your fist,' I nod thankfully, 'and let's see how hard you can hit Hattori with your knee and foot.'

I look to him in frank astonishment, my mouth doing a perfect impression of a fly trap. He must be crazy.

He claps me cheerfully on the shoulder. 'By then, I think it will be time for you to jump over the pond.'

Ninja School, Day 14
69 Days to Assassination Day

1055 hours

'The ability to keep perfectly still is the most important of the ninja's skills,' Wu instructs me. 'You, Major, must be the tree on the windless day.'

I tut and stifle a yawn. To Wu every ninja skill is the most important skill.

'If you wish to successfully ambush your enemy,' my Japanese instructor chatters on, 'it is vital he not spot you. Remember, depend on surprise, not brute strength to win the day.'

I blink but do not nod. If I do, Bee will spot it. My job is to keep perfectly still for three hours and I'm determined to pass the test.

For the second time in two weeks I'm balanced precariously on the barrel in the Rimankya Room. Wu and his clownish chum sit on pillows in front of me, chopsticks working furiously on bowls of beef and rice.

I'm hungry too, starving in fact, and my stomach growls angrily at the insult.

This is my fourteenth day of ninja school and

I'm utterly exhausted. Every hour of my seventeen hour day is now crammed full of climbing unclimbable trees, jumping unjumpable ponds and listening jadedly to Wu's non-stop summary of ninja history. In truth, not so much a summary, but the unabridged works. True, I do feel strong, and I can run faster and jump higher than a deer in a lion's den, but I'm still finding it terribly difficult to keep up.

My body is a disaster zone too, my elbows, my fists, even my knees and the bottoms of my feet cut to ribbons from pummelling poor Hattori. Mind you, my body will recover in a day or so. I don't know how and I don't know why, but it will. Thankfully, the dummy is in even worse shape than me and after almost two weeks of punching and kicking him, he is now a mere pile of matchsticks in the corner of the room.

'Time up, Major,' Wu claps his hands, 'you can stop now. Excellent work. You were most definitely the tree, though perhaps on a slightly breezy day.'

Deflated, my shoulders sink, a balloon the day after a birthday, and I clamber gingerly off the beer barrel. I feel horribly stiff, there is cramp in my legs and my stomach is howling furiously for food.

'So, what's on the menu, boys,' I joke, 'succulent pork ribs smothered in honey or, er - beef and rice?'

Wu hops to his feet. 'There'll be food shortly, Major, but first...'

He nods sharply to Bee, who, smirking callously, lumbers out of the room only to return a moment or two later lugging a second wooden dummy.

The clown plants it in front of me, his eyes cold and challenging.

'Allow me to introduce you to Hattori's brother,' Wu informs me coldly. 'Hijikata.'

A volcano erupts in my belly, red mist blurring my vision. Fourteen days of physical punishment and tiny bowls of rice and I snap. Suddenly, I do not worry if Wu and his pet clown underestimate me or not. Ignoring the urgent whispers in my skull, I storm up to the dummy and in a five second blaze of elbows, feet and fists, I reduce it to splinters.

I look to my ninja instructor, my eyes daring him to introduce me to any more of Hattori's

chiselled family.

Wu's chin drops to his chest; he eyeballs me with the sort of puzzled interest a doctor shows when he sees a particularly nasty rash. Bee, however, looks positively sickened, as if I had just murdered his pet puppy. His eyelids twitch like a bull bothered by a fly.

'I'm famished,' I mutter, flexing my battered fingers.

Recovering his composure, Wu musters up a smile. 'Food for the major it is,' his eyes narrow to tiny slots, 'or he will probably murder the cook.'

I nod. 'I probably will,' I tell him flatly, stomping off. Then, over my shoulder, 'Me and cooks, never a good mix.'

2325 hours

It is almost midnight but I simply cannot sleep. Hunger pangs rake my body and over by the window there is a rat, his tiny scampering paws ricocheting off the walls of my skull.

In my muddled, sleep-robbed mind, I see a jumble of barren rocky valleys I do not know and snowy hills I do not remember climbing. The tunnel is there too, the chanting still muffled, echoing off the roof and the icy walls.

Keen to decipher the words, I trot up the tunnel, yellow-tarnished skulls splintering under my paws, till, finally, I find myself in a gigantic cavern.

It is crowded with hooded men; rows upon rows of them like troops on parade. Over and over they chant...

They chant...

I scowl; the echo in the room is awful. It is too difficult to...

Clickety click. Clickety click. Clickety click. Bloody rat!

In a flurry of pillows and tangled blankets, I hop up off my bed and march over to the window, but the annoying rodent is nowhere to be seen.

Slamming my fist on the wall, I look out to the garden. The moon, I see, is full but then I knew it would be. The wind too cannot sleep, tossing in her bed and knocking the bananas off the trees. I can see the Chinese cracker flower by the pond, the breeze playing roughly with the...

A burst of red-hot fury thumps me in the chest and with a cry, I sink to the floor, my knees to my chin. Curled up like a baby in a womb, I pray for it to stop. I WILL DO ANYTHING! ANYTHING IF IT WILL JUST STOP.

'*Now, that is interesting*,' the demon in my mind says, slyly.

For hours, I just sit there, until finally the rat, fooled by my stillness, creeps over to investigate.

A twitch of my nose and my left eye snaps open. Then, akin to a striking python, my hand whips out and I snatch up the rodent. For a second or two, I watch it squirm and nip my thumb. Then, with a low growl, I stuff it in my mouth and begin to chew.

Ninja School, Day 29
54 Days to Assassination Day

1310 hours

Two weeks later, I'm stood in a dormitory on the top floor of Hornet Temple warily eyeing a row of bunk beds.

Wu's students, boys mostly, had returned to the temple in mid-December and I had been truly astonished to see how many he had. Young too, most of them only six or seven years old, and not only from China. Many of the labels on the trunks had Italy, Germany, even Peru or Japan written on them.

After a sixteen hour day of ninja school, they all seem to be sleeping. Seem to be, anyway, for one of them is only faking it and my job is to discover who it is before he puts a sword to my jugular.

This is my third night on the trot and so far, no luck. Or so Wu thinks. The ninja, I see, is over by the dormitory door; I think he is hoping for just a tiny bit of progress. Well, he's not going to be a happy chappy then.

In fact, I always know which boy it is, but after destroying the dummy so successfully, Wu now knows how good I am with my fists. I don't want him to discover my other skills.

I must keep the savvy ninja off-balance.

With a lantern clutched tightly in my hand, I tiptoe up to the first bed. The boy, I see, is lying on his belly and dribbling on his pillow. I smile

and skulk over to the next lumpy hill. This fellow has the raspy snore of a baby hippo, but it is a little uneven and - I scowl, my bottom lip clamped in my teeth - did I just see his nose twitch?

Cocking my head like a wary sparrow, I let my eyelids flutter shut. THUMP! THUMP! THUMP! THUMP! To me, even from six feet away, the boy's chest thunders with the urgency of a war drum. A new and very handy skill I now seem to possess.

So this is the boy, then. But I do not confront him. On the contrary, I keep my sword in my belt and creep on.

I stop by the third bed and rest my shoulder on the wall. This boy's a little older, fourteen perhaps with spotty cheeks and a nest of chins. I watch his chest; up and down, up and down. A boy in slumber; he must be in the land of nod. I look by my feet and spot his trunk, 'Jomo' handwritten in red pen on the label.

Confident this is not the lad I'm after, I pretend it is, and I press the tip of my cutlass up to his cheek. 'Got y',' I murmur. I look over to Wu but all I see is the shiny steel of a ninja short-sword.

The second bunk is now empty. As I suspected, it had been the baby hippo. The boy winks at me and with a chuckle he lowers his blade and slips off back to his bed.

Under me, Jomo's eyes flicker open and he is momentarily startled. 'Not me! Not me!' he yelps. Then he sees who it is and thankfully he seems to twig what is happening. 'The ninja skills of a humpless camel,' he murmurs sleepily. He rubs his temple, yawns and shuts his eyes.

By tomorrow, the story of my third unsuccessful attempt will be all over Hornet Temple. 'Incompetent fool!' the other students will cry. 'Why is he even here?' In fact, just what I want them to say. But they will soon discover how risky it is to think a dozing wolf has no teeth.

I pull my sword away from Jomo's cheek and slump dejectedly over to Wu. 'It's just too difficult,' I tell him, the fib slipping off my lips like jelly off a dessert spoon.

For a moment or two, he eyes me pityingly. Then with a belittling, 'TUT!' he grabs my lantern. 'I'm not a fool, Major Tor,' he says starchily.

He twirls on his heel and I watch him stomp off down the corridor. Eventually, he turns a corner and I'm left in pitch blackness.

No matter; I can see anyway. Another handy skill I now seem to possess.

Ninja School, Day 37
46 Days to Assassination Day

1145 hours, Devil's Fork

Gritting my teeth, I squeeze the tip of my foot in a cranny and lever myself up the cliff. I'm almost sixty feet up Devil's Fork, a lump of rock a mile or so west of the temple. According to Wu, a ninja must be able to climb a wall, a tree, even a cliff if he is to successfully kill his enemy. Subsequently, I spent this week clambering up bamboo ladders and perfecting the art of the ippon sugi nobori, a clever tool for shimmying up tree trunks.

And now, finally, here I am, climbing a colossal chunk of rock.

For the first time ever, I'm in full ninja garb, or shinobi shozoku in Japanese. It is a sort of tight-fitting cloth and is surprisingly robust. Unfortunately, I had not been allowed a rope and grapple for this climb, only shuko, a row of metal studs on the palms of my hands and the typical ninja split toe boot to help me grip with my feet.

My test for today is to climb the hundred and fifty feet to the top. The rock is in the shape of a three-pronged fork; I'm climbing the middle prong, Wu and Bee climb the outer two.

It is a race of sorts, a second bowl of beef and rice for the winner. I snort. Now, if it had been moose chops smothered in cloudberry sauce.

How I miss Swedish food.

Wu, I see, is almost to the top of his. Blimey! The man climbs like a scalded monkey. The clown, however, is below me, and if I keep up my speed I know I can win our private little battle. I cannot resist a tiny smirk. He will be terribly upset.

As my eyes hunt the cliff face for a hold, I wonder to myself why he detests me so much. But he is a difficult man to fathom. Had I, unknowingly, upset his mother or trod on his pet rabbit. Or, God forbid, upset his pet rabbit or trod on his mother.

'HELP ME!'

I look over my shoulder to see the clown dangling by his finger tips from a tiny outcrop of rock. If he falls he will be killed.

'BEE!' I yell. 'Try to put your foot up on the ledge.'

'I can't,' he yells back, his words drenched in terror. 'My calf's cramped up.'

It must be a fifty foot drop to the rocks below. I must get to him; Wu, I know, is too far away to help.

'Just hold on!' I cry.

I bend my knees and with a roar I jump the six feet over to Bee's pinnacle of rock. I hit the cliff so hard I almost bounce off, my fingers frantically hunting the walls for a tiny cranny or a stump of rock to grip on to.

Fiercely, I hug the cliff wall. Why do I risk my life for this numbskull, I wonder. But I know why. Even if I am possessed by demons, I'm still an officer and a man of honour, not a back alley murderer. Soon, I probably must kill Bee but it will be face to face. To let him drop after he calls for my help would be cowardly. I enjoy the challenge of being schooled by Wu but I'm still repulsed by the ninja's lack of morality.

I loosen my hold and drop nimbly to the outcrop of rock only to discover Bee on his feet next to me.

'Surprise! Surprise!'

'Oh, y' safe. Good.' But I'm annoyed. I'd just risked my life to try to help him.

I expect him to scoff but he almost blinds me with a sunny smile. My eyebrows climb my brow; I'm shocked he knows how to, that he even has teeth. It is a warning sign, a fog horn, a flashing red light, but I miss it. I'm too slow.

He kicks me brutally in the kidneys and I reel back. My feet slip from the rock and I plummet, the studs on my clawing fingers catching on the lip of the rocky outcrop.

I hang there, a fish on a fish hook soon to be skinned.

'You shouted for help,' I cry to his boots. 'I was trying to save you.'

He looks coldly down on me, his eyes bold and pitiless, unmoving to my pleas as a tombstone. 'Of course you were and that is your Achilles' heel. Tor, the typical hero, forever on the hunt for a princess to save.' He snorts. 'Trust me, Major, I'm no princess.'

'And I thought you were,' I mock him through clenched teeth. 'What with your puppy eyes and sparkling smile.' I try to swing up my foot but he kicks it maliciously away.

'This is crazy,' I hiss. 'Why bother to enrol me in your ninja school if you just intend to murder me?'

He looks up, no doubt to check Wu cannot see him. 'It is Mr Spider and Wu, not I, who wish you to be a ninja.' The words drip bitterly off his lips. 'You destroyed SWARM's plans for Norway and murdered Mr Grasshopper and Mr Locust.'

Miss Butterfly too, I think, but perhaps he had not been told.

'You cannot be trusted,' Bee snarls, 'but it seems only I can see this. It is my sworn duty to stop you.'

'But...'

'No, Major. No buts. Now, let's see if you can fly.'

My fingers crunch under the heel of his foot and my hold is lost.

I plummet silently to the rocks below.

Ninja School, Day 65
18 Days to Assassination Day

0510 hours

Proudly, I watch my elderly grandmother dig up a limp orchid in her flower bed. She must be eighty-five by now but she still looks fit and sprightly. Not a day over sixty! Every morning I see her up by five o'clock, watering and pruning her plants and replenishing the milk in the cat's bowl.

It has taken me almost two months to find her. I remember my mother telling me she lived in Ningpo but I had no clue where. My first thought had been to knock on doors but if word got back to Wu and Bee, there'd be the hell to pay. It is strictly forbidden for ninja students to go to the village.

So I had kept religiously to the woods on the outskirts of Ningpo. Every day, up with the parrots, my eyes watchful for Grandmother Toyi in the bustling throng of the village. Thankfully, a photograph of her hangs over the scullery door in my parents' house in Jokkmokk, so I know she's tiny with slim

shoulders and twinkly eyes. I know she's tiny because in the photograph she's dwarfed by a patch of sunflowers.

I had finally spotted her scattering seeds on her lawn for the birds; a tiny, stooped-over lady in a sunflower kimono and worn slippers. Even from my perch in a cypress tree, I had instantly seen in her my mother's shoulders and jaunty step.

So now, every sunup, I slip from my room in Hornet Temple, creep through the woods and sit on the handy branch to watch her.

She has a very cheeky smile and I only wish I had known her growing up.

Absentmindedly, I pick on the broken tip of my thumbnail. I only cut it yesterday but already it is annoyingly long.

My body is not the body I had before I travelled to China. Teeth now crowd my jaw, I can spot deer in the woods from half a mile away, and to me, the tiny feet of mice no longer patter, they boom like trampling elephants.

Apparently, I can also survive a fifty foot drop off a cliff with hardly a scratch and I enjoy rodents for my supper.

I feel so potent now, full of bubbling lava and

bloodthirsty tigers. I do not know if my ninja schooling is helping me to focus this energy but I do know I can jump walls and, though I'd never do it, pull up trees by the roots.

These newly discovered powers frighten me, but they electrify me too. Soon Wu will put my skills to the test and I'm confident I will pass, and when I do, I will be a ninja and a member of SWARM. Then, I will destroy this evil band of assassins once and for all.

My mind reluctantly turns to my teacher, Wu. I respect him in many ways: his mind and his formidable ninja skills, but I do not trust him. I doubt he's ever truly known love or even comradeship. He is the sort of man who will slap you warmly on the back and then put a knife in it.

In a way, I feel almost sorry for him. Almost.

I look up the hill to Hornet Temple. I spot it effortlessly; the moon is full, my eyes owlishly sharp. My nose is too, and even from here I can smell Bee's clammy 'old boot' stench. The clown is on his way to my room; my very own sadistic alarm clock.

I look longingly back to my Grandmother Toyi. I so wish to meet her, to sip lemonade, to

discuss the orchids in her flower beds and to tell her how, when I was a boy, her daughter, my mother, spoke fondly of her every day. But I cannot risk Wu seeing me with her. To him she'd be just a tool. He'd let me know, if I ever turn on him, she'd suffer.

I can never risk letting him hurt her.

Sprinting back up the hill, I tow my fingers apishly in the dirt. I don't know why I do it but it seems to help me to keep my feet when I run and not to topple over. Then I jump over the pond with the effortlessness of a deer hopping over a blade of grass. Wu still thinks I can't jump it. Better that way.

I then climb the wooden walls of the temple. A cable sprouts from the underbelly of my window sill but charily I step over it. It was put in only yesterday and, according to Wu, it is there to protect the temple from a lightning strike. But I can't see how.

Watchful of my potted orchid, I slip in the window.

With the proficient skills of a ninja warrior, I hop up on a rafter in the roof. Then, when the door opens I allow Mr Bee to walk under me. He lumbers over to my bed, his devilish-red mop of wiry curls all skew-whiff and flattened to the back of his skull. Somersaulting to the floor, I land silently and, quickly, I shut and lock the door.

No boot in the ribs for me today.

I discover Wu in the Rimankyu Room sipping kumis. I spot a second pillow on the bamboo floor. He must be expecting me, but then our six o'clock ritual chitchat is now almost three weeks old. I note there's no third pillow. I suspect he knew I'd better his thug.

'Sit, Major. Kumis is terrible for the mind but excellent for the stomach.'

Thanking him, I fold my knees, perching on the free pillow. I watch him put a match to two incense sticks, a mix of lemon and...

I sniff the curling smoke.

...cherry wood?

'No Mr Bee,' Wu begins. I spot deep shadows under his eyes. I suspect my tutor did not sleep too well. 'I can only presume then that you locked him in your room.' He balloons his cheeks. 'That's every day this week. He will be awfully upset.'

I nod. The smell from the sticks is potent and I feel my eyelids begin to droop. 'Then Mr Bee

must find a different spot to park his boot in the mornings.'

The ninja smirks and drinks from his tumbler. He understands cruel humour. 'Indeed he must.'

I feel almost comfortable with this man now. Uncomfortably so, for I know he is a murderer, a man of no morality, in his words, 'A fly to be swotted'.

'You told me you were born in Japan,' I suddenly blurt out, 'so why is your ninja school here, in China?'

He eyes me thoughtfully and I'm confident he will not tell me. He's a ninja, after all. A man of secrets. Then, suddenly, his lips curl up. 'When I was just a boy of six, my father packed me and my two brothers off to the best ninja school on our island.'

He's whispering now and I wonder why. Is he frightened there's a spy in Hornet Temple? But if there is, who is he and who's he spying for?

'In a matter of months I could shoot arrows, climb walls and purposefully dislocate my shoulder to slip free of a knotted rope.

'Then, on my 16th birthday, I was honoured

with the job of murdering the owner of a rival ninja school. My final test. If I succeeded, I'd be Genin, a ninja agent.'

'Did you do it?'

'If I had not, Major, I very much doubt I'd be sitting here telling you the story.

'Unfortunately, there was a boy in my school who was very upset he had not been chosen for this honourable mission. In a fit of rage, he went to the rival school and told them who had committed the murder. So, I chopped off the boy's tongue and my family went on the run. Eventually, we escaped to China.'

Blimey! This is not a man to cross, which is a little disconcerting as I totally intend to cross him.

Wu rubs his eyes, perhaps trying to rub away the memory.

'So your brothers left Japan with you?'

'Yes, and no. My younger brother did; he now works for SWARM, but my elder brother, he er, well, he decided to stay. I do not know what happened to him.'

'And then you met up with SWARM and set up this school in Hornet Temple?' I ask.

Like a stepped-on cobra, the tip of his tongue

darts to his lips. My interest in him is making him jumpy. 'Major Tor, I will tell you the rest of my life story the day I trust you.'

'When I pass the ninja test and I'm a Genin too?'

'No.' He smirks evilly, his eyes full of secrets. 'Then SWARM will trust you. I'm ninja, I trust nobody.'

I shrug indifferently, shifting a little on my numb bottom. How terrible it must be to spend your days trusting nobody. No wonder he drinks so much; the bottle is there to keep him company.

'You impress me, Major,' Wu chews thoughtfully on his bottom lip, 'yet you confuse me too. You climb like a monkey and your skill with the sword is almost superhuman; I still wonder how it is you were not killed when you fell from Devil's Fork. No cuts, not even a broken bone. To put it mildly, Mr Bee was very upset.'

'I bet,' I snarl. 'The snake attempted to murder me.'

'No! No!' His eyebrows arch hawkishly. 'He just plays a little rough.'

I snort and violently stir my drink with a

finger.

'But for all my tutoring, you still will not jump the pond and you insist you cannot tell who is asleep and who is not. I wonder if, perhaps, my student is not trying to trick me.' He puts his hands together as if in prayer. 'Possibly you wish me to underestimate you. If this is so, then you underestimate me.'

Widening my eyes innocently, I sip from my tumbler. The kumis, a mildly alcoholic drink fermented from cows' milk, is thick and creamy. Wu drinks too, his third glassful.

The ninja rubs his chin thoughtfully then blankly tells me, 'Gojo-Goyuko.'

I scowl. 'That's the name of SWARM's ship, is it not?'

'Bravo, Major. And...'

Oh! He expects me to know what it actually is. 'Venom,' I propose tentatively, 'or a, er, blowfish soup...'

'No, Major,' he sucks in his cheeks, 'it is the Japanese word for the study of the flaws of the enemy.'

'Oh, yes. I see.' I nod wisely, trying to look as if this would have been my third guess.

Wu rubs his temple and ploughs on. 'If the

enemy is a coward, or too kind perhaps, or maybe just has a terribly short temper, a clever ninja can turn this on him, exploiting his Achilles' heel.' Wu's eyes twinkle. He enjoys sermonising. 'Using a bribe, flattery or a well thought out insult, the ninja can prod the enemy into doing whatever he wants him to do. You see, Major, by understanding the enemy's flaws, he can be easily manipulated and controlled. That is Gojo-Goyuko.'

I steeple my fingers under my chin and mull his words over. Bee had told me on Devil's Fork what my Achilles' heel is: the need to help, to be the hero, and his knowledge of it had almost killed me.

Wu sighs audibly and begins to suck on his teeth. He often reminds me of his philosophy degree from Oxford and my inability to instantly accept his wisdom annoys him immensely. 'Allow me to offer an example,' he mutters, frustration echoing in his words.

I nod. Wu is a monster, but he's also a very talented storyteller and his fanciful yarns usually keep me rooted to my pillow. He swills his mouth with kumis and then swallows; he also drinks too much.

'A powerful ninja is given the responsibility of murdering thirteen of his master's political opponents. Now, this assassin is a very intelligent chap. He looks down the list and sees Lord Nin Po is on there, third from the bottom. The ninja knows this lord to be a very kindly sort and very popular with his followers. He also knows if he is to succeed and kill all thirteen men on his list, he must murder Nin Po first.'

My storyteller cocks his eyebrow and I nod my understanding so far.

'So, the ninja, confident in Nin Po's kindly ways, sits by the door to his castle and pretends to be a leper. The next day, on his way to temple, the lord spots the leper, walks over to him and drops a penny in his lap. The ninja jumps up and thanks him with the swipe of his sword. The assassin then allows himself to be captured and under torture, he surrenders his twelve co-conspirators.'

He looks to me with a quizzical eyebrow.

Reluctantly, I nod. 'They were not his twelve co-conspirators, they were his other twelve targets.' I see the logic in the ninja's plan but still there is no honour in trickery.

'Just so!' Wu claps his hands, no doubt misinterpreting my understanding for agreement. 'The clever ninja knew how much the lord's followers adored him and he correctly judged they'd avenge his murder. They did the rest of the ninja's job for him.'

'I admit it's a clever ploy,' I murmur, 'but it's still cowardly.'

'No, Major,' Wu counters with a flaring of his nostrils, 'not cowardly, smart. Remember, only emperors can enjoy the luxury of morals, ninjas can only ever enjoy beef stew and cold beds.'

'Honour is important too,' I snap back crossly, 'even to a ninja. The lion is worshipped, not the cheetah.'

'Perhaps, but the cheetah brings terror and with terror there is respect.'

'I think maybe Sensei Wu is confusing respect with...'

Annoyingly, Wu shows me the mollifying palms of his hands. 'Major, we can ponder the ins and outs of morality tomorrow. Now, however, we must look to our job for today.' He hops athletically to his feet and, crossly, I scramble up to follow him, bringing my drink with me. It seems, in Hornet Temple anyway, his word is law. There is no room for debate. I wonder, perhaps, if he is frightened I will find a gaping hole in his cold, hard logic.

He escorts me over to a low bench. On it there is a hotchpotch of ninja equipment: I spot a rope and grapple, a pile of throwing stars, even a few caltrops or tetsubishi: sharp metal barbs which, if thrown on the floor, will impale the feet of any unsuspecting enemy. Very nasty!

On the floor, under the bench, I spy two small wooden barrels. Wu shows them to me. 'Your excellent bible tells us Jesus can walk on water,' he whispers. 'Well, so can ninja and I will show you how to.

'But first, I have important news.' Then he drops his bombshell. 'Tomorrow you and I will travel to Beijing to meet Empress Cixi, the ruler of China.'

I blink in surprise. He says it so calmly: 'Just off to the shops, Old Fellow' but, despite his unruffled manner, I still suspect this is root of his Panda-blackened eyes.

'The city is far to the north so we will journey by ship on the Grand Canal.' The

corners of his lips curl up. 'Cixi is a stickler for ceremony, Major, so I strongly recommend you iron your uniform and polish your boots.'

Many days on a ship with only Wu and his boorish clown for company. 'Wonderful news,' I utter in palpable dismay.

'Good.' My bad mood is lost on him. Finishing off his drink, he swaps his tumbler for the two barrels. 'Now, to work. But first, Major, go and unlock the door to your room. We don't want Mr Bee to smash it in, do we?'

'No, Sensei.' And with a forced smile, I down the rest of my drink too.

2315 hours

On this cold January night, my nightmare returns. I'm back in the cave; it is still wall to wall with hooded men but now, finally, I comprehend the words. 'Skufsi Tennur!' they chant. 'Skufsi Tennur!'

Slowly, I walk by them, the skulls under my paws no longer ivory-white but blood-red and sticky. A demon's red carpet.

I do not know why, but I know this crowd of

men will not hurt me. Indeed, the closest of them, when they see me, begin to bow. The rest soon follow; a ripple in a pond when a pebble is thrown in.

Why, I wonder, and where is this Skufsi Tennur, this wolf they chant for? Did I not kill it; slay it with Tyrfing's steel?

But, for now, they bow to me. A growl swells my chest...

They bow to Tor.

Monday, 24th January, 1872
11 Days to Assassination Day

1215 hours, Grand Canal

Our taxi, or chuzu qiche, is a ship called 'Gulong', Chinese for 'Old Dragon'. She must be thirty or so feet from bow to stern; she has two masts, a tiny windowless cabin - where my uniform and boots sit ironed and polished - and even a loo. Well, sort of. A hole in the floor anyway. I'm surprised by how nippy she is, but then I remember the rifle Astrid Solbakken's impostor had had in Stockholm. Perhaps this

ship has been cleverly altered too.

The skipper's name is Yi. He looks very old to me, melancholy showing in the folds of his skin. His back is bent over like a tree in a storm, his cheeks smothered in liver spots and he always has on a furry pelt cap. He keeps his eyes to narrow slits, tired perhaps of looking out on such a cruel world.

It is a wintry day, a bitingly cold wind nipping my fingers and trying to flip up the hem of my robe. Wu and I sit drinking coffee in the bow of the ship but I can still see Yi and his son by the wheel in the stern. Our skipper is obviously an expert on the rudder, skilfully slipping in and out of, but never over, the hundreds of tiny rafts littering the canal.

His son, Qin, is nine and I spot him cooking food by his father's feet. He drops corn cobs in the pot and slowly stirs it.

A pebble hits my shoulder and I look over to the culprit, Wu. 'Tomorrow we will be in Beijing,' he tells me flatly.

I nod happily. This is excellent news. We've been on the ship for almost a week and I'm in need of a hot bath, a bed not a hammock, and very different company.

'There, in the rooms of the Forbidden City, we will meet Empress Cixi.'

'Cixi,' I murmur, mulling over the word. 'Such a fluffy name.'

Wu shrugs. 'She's anything but fluffy. She's got the claws of a tiger and the temper of a rattle snake.'

I shift my bottom; Tyrfing's hilt is digging into my ribs. 'You know her then,' I say matter-of-factly.

'Nobody knows the empress,' he corrects me. 'But I met her when I did a job for her many years ago. She is the absolute ruler of the Manchu Qing Dynasty and all of China. I will tell you of her; it is important to know your enemy.' He smirks. 'Remember Gojo-Goyuko and the Devil's Fork.'

I chew on my lip. It is a bitter memory. 'Is she my enemy then?'

'No, not today anyway. But tomorrow, who knows? Remember, Major, even a brother is often just the enemy in the wings.'

Miss Butterfly, Astrid Solbakken's impostor, springs to mind and I ruefully nod. I still think of her. Not often, but, well - she had the most wonderful eyes.

I often wonder 'what if'. I know I'm not the most dishy of fellows: the cut on my cheek; the fact I smell of wet dog. But my jaw is sort of chiselled and a girl in France - admittedly, she had been a little tipsy - did tell me I had the shoulders of a lumberjack.

What if I had not shot the wonderfully clever, wonderfully pretty assassin? What if...

'In 1851,' Wu begins, interrupting my wistful thoughts, 'when Cixi was only sixteen, she was chosen for the Emperor's bed to be his concubine. Together, they had a boy, Tongzhi, the Emperor's only son.

'Then, ten years later, in 1861 the Emperor fell terribly ill and left this world. His doctors insisted he suffered a heart attack, but...' He stops and sips thoughtfully from his cup.

I frown. There is a secret there, but I do not press him.

'Cixi immediately had the Emperor's old ministers executed and took over the country. She is the only empress of the Qing Dynasty and the only empress ever to be the ruler of China.'

And I must meet her. My lips feel swollen and dry and I sip from my cup too, scalding my tongue.

'Cixi is incredibly powerful,' Wu explains to me. He speaks slowly, stressing every word. 'She's almost a god here in China and she's incredibly sly too. Her son, Tongzhi, however, who will soon be emperor, is not. He's a drunk and a bad-tempered fool. If he is there, be watchful of him.'

I nod. I'm watchful of everybody.

My belly growls in mutiny and I wonder, absentmindedly, why I'm always so hungry. On cue, the skipper's son, Qin, tromps over and hands us bowls, chopsticks for Wu and a spoon for me. I peer in keenly: chicken stir-fry, rice, chopped carrots and a cob of corn. Hurray! No beef stew.

'Xiexie,' I utter, Chinese for 'thank you'.

'Oh, yes,' Wu nods, 'Mr Bee told me your mother is Chinese.'

'He knows too much,' I spit, happy we had left the brute back in the temple.

'He's a member of SWARM,' the Japanese ninja counters. 'They tend to know everything.' Thoughtfully, he picks at a scab on his knee. 'Your mother still has family in China perhaps?'

'I don't know,' I fib recklessly. I must protect my Grandmother Toyi from this monster's claws. I shovel chicken in my mouth and try unobtrusively to switch topics. 'So, do you know why this Empress Cixi is so keen to meet with us?'

'Sort of,' he splutters, spitting rice. His mouth is now full of food too, his chopsticks a blur. 'In the empress's wisdom, she allowed SWARM to set up the ninja school here in China. We pay her amply but to keep her happy we do the odd job for her too.'

'So she probably needs us to chop up her Uncle Jimmy,' I joke, 'or her wrinkly old granny.'

I spot the involuntary twitch of Wu's left eye followed by a disapproving sniff. He is not particularly a fan of my brand of humour. 'Perhaps,' he admits eventually. 'But know this, Major, whatever the job is, no matter how dangerous, you will be doing it.'

'ME!'

He smirks, his eyes hard and uncompromising. 'It will be the final test of your ninja skills and knowledge. Then, upon your success, you will be Genin, a ninja agent.

You can join the ranks of SWARM and be told all of her secrets.'

I chew thoughtfully on my cob of corn and watch China drift slowly by. It seems, according to the Gulong's skipper, the Grand Canal is over 1,700km long. It connects Beijing in the north to the city of Hangzhou in the south and many parts of it date back to 400BC.

It is truly wonderful, the country, not the corn. A land of open forests, hills and towering craggy rocks. I spot a donkey lugging a cart of straw, and a camel, his humps enveloped in rolls upon rolls of blankets. Old stooping men carry wicker baskets on bony shoulders and a pig follows docilely on the heels of a tiny boy.

A junk, a sort of Chinese trawler with a cheery-red hull and a chunky rudder, sits just off our bow. The men on the poop deck look sullen and moody; cold too by the look of it, cocooned in lumpy woollen rugs. Perhaps not the most successful of fishing days.

'Unfortunately,' Wu ploughs on, 'to see the empress we must enter her palace in the Forbidden City.'

'Unfortunately?' I echo him, lifting my eyebrows.

He props his chin on his fist. 'Usually, the royal family do not allow non-Chinese in there.' Dropping his bowl to the deck he burps. 'Remember to keep your eyes to your feet, bow low and never, ever show Cixi or her son your back.'

I'm sorely tempted to roll my eyes. Wu's overdoing it a bit, but yet, my belly suddenly feels awfully hollow. I remedy the problem by stuffing a spoonful of rice in it.

'It is important, Major Tor, to show Empress Cixi the utmost respect and follow the customs of the palace.' He taps his chopsticks on the deck, emphasising his next words. 'You see, she has this annoying tendency to chop off the feet of anybody who upsets her.'

'How sweet,' I drone gloomily. 'Can I keep my boots?' With a growling tummy, I drop the spoon in the empty bowl; I am still terribly hungry but it seems in China chicken stir-fry is no different to beef stew.

Then...

I shudder and I feel my back involuntarily arch. The drum of six chests. LUB DUB! LUB DUB! LUB DUB! The stench of arrogance and...

I sniff.

Bee's wax, I think grimly, perfect for polishing swords.

The ship staggers and with a snarl, I spring to my feet, my sword, Tyrfing, clutched in my fist. Wu jumps up too but he seems a little wobbly and elbows over his cup. Coffee splatters the deck. I scowl. It looks too milky to be...

I eye my tutor, his ruddy cheeks, the tremor of his little finger. Damn! The man's drunk.

Clinging to the hope we only hit a submerged rock, my eyes cut to the front of the ship. The junk I spotted is now stern to bow with us, tiny steel anchors roping her to the jib boom. Stonily, I watch six oddly-dressed men scuttle over a row of planks and thump to the Gulong's deck.

Not a rock then.

Swathed in black - the rugs now thrown to the wind - with horned helmets and dragon masks, they look like monsters from a horror story. But I can still see the eyes. Stony cold. Killers. Men with a job to do. But still, just men.

'Samurai,' mutters Wu ominously. 'The

enemy of the ninja.'

He steps back and I wonder for a moment if he's going to abandon me and jump ship. But in a split second, the enemy surround us. Wu is too slow. A worrying thought considering our predicament.

In a flurry of wolfish barks, they charge. I duck under a sweeping sword, twist and elbow my attacker ruthlessly in the stomach. Wheezing, he bends over and I wallop the back of his skull with the hilt of my sword.

Wu, I see, is still on his feet fending off three of the enemy. I hurry over to help him but then a second samurai jumps me. This fellow is colossal with the stumpy legs of a rhino. His sword sweeps up, grazing the cleft of my chin. I scurry back but he doggedly follows me, jabbing relentlessly for my chest. He is a hunter and he can smell my blood. I block his thrusts and with a howl of fury, I suddenly step up to him and bustle him up and off the deck. He plummets to the water below.

The swish of steel and I instinctively duck, a shimmering sword skewering the barrel by my shoulder. My third attacker yanks on the hilt trying to wrench it free but it is jammed in the timber.

In the past, I'd do the man the civility of stepping off; he'd been unlucky and that is no way to win a fight. But not now. Not today. Today, I cuff him brutally on the jaw.

A volcano spits and growls in my chest, pummelling my rib cage. I see my blurred eyes in the back of the blade, they burn yellow, and fervently I look for the next man to brawl.

My eyes flit to my tutor. I spot two samurai slumped by his feet but the third is doing considerably better, handling his sword with expert hands. I can tell Wu is tiring; too many cups of kumis.

'*Throw the sword.*' The demon is back. It knows my instincts, my primal instincts. '*Be all you can be,*' it bellows in my skull. '*THROW IT NOW!*'

So I do. I pull the sword from the barrel, the outstretched blade quivering in fury, and with all the venom I can muster, I let fly. It tomahawks over the deck, hitting Wu's attacker with such ferocity, he is thrown twenty feet, landing with a bone-crunching thud on the cabin roof.

With fury simmering under my skin, I storm

over to the body. I must...

'*Yes. Yes, you must.*'

...claw open his chest. Gnaw on his ribs.

'*Don't forget the liver, lots of iron in liver. It will keep you strong.*'

I must...

'*FEED ON HIM!*'

I drop to my knees and rip open the samurai's tunic. But then, new words spiral in my mind. Softer. Dampening the fury. They block the demon's playful temptings and slowly, I slump to the deck.

'*Rest now,*' the angel tells me, so I do.

1610 hours, The Forbidden City

Wu and I stand stamping our feet and rubbing our hands by the south wall of the Forbidden City. It is a bitterly cold afternoon in the Chinese capital of Beijing and I'm happy to be back in my woollen cavalry uniform. Though, I must admit, after three months in China, I now kind of miss my comfy ninja robe.

By my elbow is a gigantic archway in the

wall. A tiny Chinese lady in chunky-heeled clogs and a sunflower dress scampers through it, spots us and clip-clops over.

I look her over and shiver. She must be awfully cold.

'Konichiwa, Wu-san.' I think this is Japanese for 'Hello, Mr Wu'. She knows Japanese then; a woman of talents. She bows deeply, her eyes to his. I scowl. There is, I think, an air of familiarity between them. 'Welcome to the Forbidden City,' she tells him.

'Thank you.' He bows too then nods to me. 'This is Major Tor.'

'Hello, Major,' she says in perfectly clipped English.

I bow stiffly and she mirrors me, her lips set to 'unhappy moon'. She reminds me a little of a sad porcelain doll.

'My name is Soo Po and my job today is to show you a little of the palace and to escort you to Empress Cixi.'

She lifts her eyebrows expectantly so we nod.

'Good. Do follow me and, er, try to keep up. There's lots to see.'

Obediently, we chase her flapping heels through the archway to a gigantic cobbled

square. I immediately spot a winding river lined with gnarled cypress trees, and on a far off terrace, three towering wooden halls.

'The Forbidden City, or Zijin Cheng, is the home of China's empress,' Soo Po begins our schooling. 'Surrounded by a wall twenty-six feet high and twenty feet thick, it was built by Emperor Zhu Di of the Ming Dynasty between 1406 and 1420 and it is by far the biggest palace in the world.' There then follows a dramatic pause. 'It has almost 9,000 rooms and took...'

'I see every roof is yellow,' I interrupt her monologue.

'Yes,' she snaps. I can tell she is in no mood to extend the history lesson. 'It is the colour of the empress.

'It took almost fifteen years to construct the palace,' she tutors on. 'Phoebe zhennan wood for the walls, marble for the terrace and baked bricks from the city of Suzhou for the floors.

'Then, in 1644 the Ming Dynasty ended in a bloody battle and Shunnzhi, the very first Qing emperor, was crowned here, in the Forbidden City.'

We follow her over a bridge, serpents carved into the wood, to a second square. I burrow my hands in my armpits to try to shelter my frosty fingers from the bitter winds. I think there must be crystals frosting my whiskers.

'This river is called Inner Golden Water,' Soo Po enlightens us. 'It flows throughout the Forbidden City.' Then she nods to the three halls. 'And here you can see the Hall of Supreme Harmony, the Hall of Central Harmony and the Hall of Preserving Harmony.'

'I think I can detect a theme here,' I whisper to Wu.

But the ninja pays my jesting no heed whatsoever. He's far too jumpy. The attack on our ship spooked him. Well, I think it did. He's not spoken of it, not even to thank me for saving his skin. Embarrassed perhaps and probably a little humiliated.

We trot up a set of smooth marble steps and through the archway of the grandest of the three halls. There, I follow Wu and Soo Po's example, and slip off my boots.

'Empress Cixi will meet you here, in the Hall of Supreme Harmony.' Soo Po throws me a quizzical look. 'You must be very important. This hall is the hub of China's spiritual and

political power. Usually only royalty is allowed in here.'

It is, I must admit, very impressive in a minimalist sort of way. Everything but for the golden-bricked floor is wooden: the roof, the doors, even the borders of the papery walls, but oddly there is no furniture, no intricately carved cabinets, no gilt-edged chests, not even a tiny petal-dyed vase or a throne.

I wonder, idly, what Cixi sits on.

In fact, the only object in the hall is a gigantic wooden Buddha. I can tell by the smell it's been chiselled from a sandalwood tree; a woodsy, spicy summer smell with a hint of nutmeg. The scent of it fills the room. Heavenly!

'Why is it called the Forbidden City?' I ask Soo Po.

She shrugs. 'It is forbidden for commoners to enter it. In the olden days, if commoners inadvertently set eyes on the emperor, they were executed on the spot. So we stopped letting them in.'

I can tell by her stony glower she thinks I'm very much the commoner and she much prefers the 'olden day' rule - if only for today.

'I will inform the empress of your arrival,'

she says. 'Stay here.' She bows, adding, 'And don't play with anything.'

I scowl, my eyes wandering the hall. There's nothing much to play with, I want to tell her but I bite my tongue.

I catch her throw Wu a nervy look, then she pitter-pats off and I'm left with a very twitchy ninja.

'Now, remember what I told you,' he mutters nervously.

'I will,' I comfort him.

'To bow.'

'Yes.'

'To always address her, Empress...'

'Yes.'

'...and to never, ever contradict her.'

'Of course, Sensei. I will show her the respect I show you.'

'Hmm.' He puckers up his lips. 'That, Major, is what is worrying me.'

I'm surprised by how jittery Wu is. He's supposed to be the unflappable, cucumber-cool ninja but, in fact, he reminds me of a boy in a schoolmaster's study in trouble for pulling little Jemima's pigtails.

I look up to the beamed roof and spot the

intricate carving of a dragon, shiny silver orbs erupting from the jaws...

'Major,' spits Wu and I feel his urgent pinch on my skin.

Apprehensively, I drop my eyes to watch a slightly butch Chinese lady with a chalk-powdered face march purposefully in the door. By my elbow, Wu bows. This must be Empress Cixi, so I hastily copy him.

'I do not usually meet with commoners,' she informs us blankly in English, stopping just short of Wu, 'but our words today must be spoken in the utmost secrecy. Even my son must not know.' She coldly eyeballs the ninja. 'My darling husband, the Xianfeng Emperor, left this world ten years ago with a little help from you, Ninja.' She smirks. 'You did an adequate job for me then.'

'I was honoured to be of help, My Empress.'

'Undoubtedly, but you never told me how you did it.' She eyes him greedily; an owl watching a field mouse.

Wu looks almost coy. 'A ninja never tells his secrets...'

'Wu,' she snaps.

The ninja quickly relents, rattling off, 'Two

spoons of hemlock in his whisky and a golden dart frog in his pyjamas.'

The frogs in Wu's pond!

'Clever,' she spits, with a witch's cackle. 'His doctors told me he shook so much he bit off his tongue.'

I'm deeply shocked. It seems Wu murdered Empress Cixi's husband, the emperor of China, and his butch wife actually ordered the ninja to do it!

'This is Major Tor.' Wu flaps a nervy hand at me. 'He is also a ninja, or he soon will be if he keeps up the good work.'

She cuts her eyes to me and I feel my skin prickle under her cold gaze. 'Trustworthy too, I hope,' she says with the hint of a sneer.

'Completely, Empress. He's almost family.' He pats me in a brotherly way on the shoulder as if to prove it.

I know Cixi is only thirty-six, Wu told me, but she looks considerably older to me. She has a hard jaw, deeply cold eyes and a squashed boxer's nose. Pink slippers peek out from under the hem of her long gown and I see she is holding a pretty yellow fan. My jaw drops and I blink. One of the nails on her left hand must be

over a foot long.

'For twenty years, the Qing Dynasty has battled the rebels,' she tells us. 'In November, I thought my general, Li Fuzhong, with the help of the British army had destroyed the last of them, but now, it seems, there is rumour of a new rebel boss, the traitor, Yixin.'

'I see,' Wu nods, 'and you wish for SWARM to assist you in...'

'I wish for Yixin to depart this world, the sooner the better.' Cixi directs her cobra eyes to Wu, her balled-up fist on her hip. 'And I expect SWARM to help him to pack.'

I wince. There is no hiding the venom in her metaphor.

The ninja bows so deeply, his chin almost hits his knees. 'For you, Empress, anything.'

'Excellent. My son, Tongzhi, will soon be emperor and he is not,' she sighs resignedly, 'the cleverest of boys. It is very important to China he never face Yixin and his band of rebels.

'Succeed in this task, Ninja, and I will allow SWARM to keep the school in Hornet Temple for a further ninety-nine years.' The corner of her mouth twists up shrewdly. 'However, if you fail me, I will instruct my General Li to toss you and your ninjas into the South China Sea. Understood?'

'Understood, Empress Cixi.' Wu has turned so green, I wonder if he has just swallowed a bad clam.

Now she steps up to me and I shiver. She eyes me disdainfully. 'Tell me, Wu, why is Major Tor even here?'

'He will soon be a very powerful ninja,' Wu enlightens her to my utmost surprise; it seems all my efforts not to show off my skills were unsuccessful. 'It will be his job to, er,' he swallows, perhaps trying to find the words, 'carry out your orders.'

She looks me over for just a second but it seems to go on forever and I begin to feel like an insect under a magnifying glass. Possibly she is wondering if I'm trustworthy or not and I instinctively lift my chin. 'I see there is Chinese blood in you, Major,' she says icily.

'Yes.' I nod, a little surprised by her keen eye. 'My mother.'

'Hmm,' she taps the spindly nail on the tip of her cauliflower nose, 'and she is still in China, in Beijing perhaps?'

'No, she's in Sweden with my father.'

'Sweden, you say.' She furrows her ivory-powered brow. 'Oh yes, I remember now, it is a city in Switzerland. They sell cuckoo clocks there and puffins sleep in the trees.'

'Actually, no,' I correct her with a tiny chuckle. 'Sweden's a country to the north of Germany. Puffins,' I scratch my chin, 'I think they mostly live in Iceland, and cuckoo clocks, well...'

I'm stopped by the elbow and angry hiss of Wu. Suddenly, I feel Cixi's irritation crowding in on me; an elephant's foot on my shoulders. Perhaps now is not the moment to tell her how, in Sweden, I threw a bowl of broth at a cuckoo clock.

'A country, you say,' the empress snarls with a flare of her nostrils. 'If I do not know it, then it must be very, very small.'

'It is,' I nod enthusiastically, keen for her not to chop off my feet, 'compared to the wonder and power of China.'

'If it is so tiny then I'm correct, it is just a city. A tiny city.'

She is being so monstrously stupid, all I can think to stutter is, 'Er, no...'

'Yes Empress, it must be,' Wu interrupts me. 'In fact, perhaps it's only a town or a village.'

'It's a city, Wu,' she snaps, her words bullyish and sharp, her eyes crackling with electricity.

'Yes! Yes!' I feel the ninja's elbow in my ribs. 'It must be. It is! It is!'

This is ridiculous; the empress of China is barmy, a tankard short of a barrel, but remembering my vow to Wu, I swallow my pride and with only a splinter of scorn, I mumble, 'Yes, Sweden's a city.'

'Excellent.' Her eyes glitter triumphantly. 'We all agree then.'

I'm stunned. Empress Cixi is so confident in her godly powers, she thinks whatever she decrees to be true will be magically so.

'Now, to work. You will find Yixin in his castle in Wuxi, a town,' she throws me a malevolent look, daring me to quarrel with her, 'on the Tai Hu Lake. It is perhaps only a two days ride from your temple.'

Her eyes soften slightly. 'Yixin is an extraordinary man and very intelligent too, so do not underestimate him, Major. I was told of the attack on your ship. Yixin probably sent

them. He knows then of my plan to send assassins and, consequently, I expect there will be many guards and a number of clever and very nasty booby traps. Yixin himself is an excellent swordsman.'

'I must applaud you, Empress Cixi,' Wu bleats sheepishly. 'You know your enemy well. It is the ninja way: Goyo-Goyuko.'

'It is hardly a difficult chore.' She folds up the fan with a gunshot snap and slaps it on her open palm. 'The disloyal scum happens to be my brother-in-law.'

The temperature in the hall drops markedly and I shiver.

I see Wu frown. I know this man now and I can tell by the shuffle of his feet this is not the best of news.

'Perhaps,' says the ninja timidly, 'with such a risky job, I should...'

'No!' snaps Cixi. 'Major Tor will do it. I insist. He's insolent but I need a man with backbone to murder Yixin, not a wobbly jelly who kills by putting frogs in pyjamas.'

Thin-lipped, Wu nods. 'I see.'

'I very much doubt you do,' the empress mutters sneeringly.

The ninja swallows, the blood emptying from his cheeks like sand from an hourglass. Oh my! He's actually hopping from foot to foot. Now I'm seeing his true colours. The tough warrior is just a shell. Under it he is just a cowardly buffoon.

'Wu,' snaps Cixi, 'if you need the loo...'

'No, no, I er...'

'Then be off,' she flaps her fan at us, 'and I expect to hear the sad news of Yixin's death very soon. Oh, and Major Tor, remember this, if you do not succeed, the only apology I will accept will be your severed feet on a silver platter.'

I swallow my own fear and nod. 'I completely understand,' I say, trying to keep the jitters from distorting my words. She may be the ruler of China but in my mind she's also a total and utter psychopath.

I bow deeply, and with the shaking Wu on my elbow, we back-pedal from the room.

Monday, 1st February, 1872
3 Days to Assassination Day

0925 hours, Ningpo

I rest my shoulder on the papery thin door to my Grandmother Toyi's house and ponder what to do next.

I so wish to meet her. I'm tired of the ugly company I keep: Wu, Bee, the crazy empress and the school of ninja, boys who should be playing with clockwork toys, not swords and caltrops. I desperately need an ally in this world of murderers I find myself in.

I know Wu is up in the temple meeting privately with Bee, so there is hardly any chance I will be seen. But I worry I will frighten Grandmother or my Chinese will be too awful for her to comprehend my words.

I scowl and rub my throbbing temple.

The return trip to Hornet Temple had taken almost a week and during it, Wu and I had hardly spoken a word, the ninja preferring the company of a bottle of kumis to me.

And I know why.

He knows I know his flaw, his Goyo-

Goyuko: the hot tempered and highly volatile Empress Cixi. She has the power to shut down Hornet Temple and he's uncomfortable that I know it. On top of that, the future of SWARM in China now rests in my hands.

I can hardly blame him for being so jumpy and I wonder nervously if he suspects I intend to destroy his school and stop the conveyor belt of new ninja to SWARM. And that I plan for Empress Cixi to unwittingly help me to do it.

I will effectively be cutting off SWARM's blood supply.

But to destroy this evil organization, I must storm the castle of Empress Cixi's brother-in-law, Yixin, and murder him. Or so it must seem. Only then will Wu trust me with SWARM's secrets.

Knowledge is power!

Then I plan to pack up and travel back to England.

The assassin, Granny Moth, had told me in the tunnels under Stockholm's Royal Castle that the prince of Denmark had a spy in SWARM's London camp, and I suspect Spider, the elusive boss of SWARM, is in London too. I just spent twelve months trying to infiltrate the

HQ there with no luck at all, but now, this job for Empress Cixi is my way in.

The kettle in Grandmother's house begins to whistle insistently. I almost knock but I stop, my fist hovering over the wood.

I know my Grandmother Toyi knows me - well, of me. When I was growing up in Jokkmokk, my mother sent her a letter every month and every month a letter dropped in the letterbox from Grandmother, a woman I had never even met.

I remember as a boy I sat on my mother's lap trying to decipher the oddly-shaped Chinese letters. My mother had helped me and I had discovered in my grandmother's writing a world of blood orchids, bamboo trees and Chinese cracker flowers. My ma's letters had in turn been full of me and my little sister, Sylva.

My parents had met in Shanghai in the summer of 1845. Back then my father had been a skipper on a cotton ship and it had docked in China to pick up fresh cargo. They had met in a café; my mother worked there and had accidentally spilt coffee in my father's lap.

When my father told me this story he insisted she had spilt the coffee purposefully just to meet him. But I remember my mother just rolling her eyes and with a tiny impish smile patting him affectionately on the shoulder.

Anyway, purposefully or not, he had been instantly smitten by her.

Back then, a rebel uprising threatened to overrun Shanghai and bring down the Emperor and the Qing Dynasty. So, my father, frightened they'd be killed if they stayed in China, smuggled my mother back to Sweden.

I know my mother desperately missed Grandmother but in 1845 there was no Suez Canal and the voyage took almost four months, way too long a trip for a women on her own. Anyway, my father's ship no longer travelled to China.

Suddenly, the door springs open and a very old lady looks up at me. She has cottony curls and a basket of cut flowers in her hand. 'I see you in that tree every morning watching me,' she tells me blankly. I frown, trying to follow her Chinese words. 'I may be old but I'm not blind. So, if you plan to rob me...'

She falters and her lips pucker up. 'On my window sill there is a picture of a boy,' she says

slowly. 'He's only six and I never met him but he has my eyes. And so do you,' she frowns, 'but for the...'

'Hello Grandmother Toyi,' I say simply.

'Tor,' she whispers, dropping the basket of flowers.

I step up to her and hug her to my chest.

~

I sit on my grandmother's patched-up sofa, my eyes travelling the room. It is a little cramped and a little cluttered, but after the cold hard décor of the Forbidden City and Hornet Temple, it feels wonderfully cosy. I see flowers everywhere in crooked-looking pots, and over in the corner by a bookshelf there sits a potter's wheel and a stool. It seems Grandmother Toyi has a hobby.

I spy a Chinese cracker flower on the window sill, and just by it, the silver-framed photograph of a boy. Me, by the look of it. A very cheerful-looking me.

Soft fur rubs my foot and I look down to see a black cat under the coffee table. I scratch involuntarily and tut. By tomorrow my chest will be a puzzle of ugly red welts.

The cat and I lock eyes and I find myself idly pondering the different ways of cooking it. Skewer it, dip it in lemon then grill it, or, even better, put it in a curry or a chilli on a bed of honey-glazed carrots. Or, perhaps, just chew it raw. A glob of drool drips down onto the cleft of my chin. Suddenly, with a high-pitched meow, the cat jumps up and scarpers from the room.

I rest back on the sofa and wonder if Grandmother's furry pet has the ability to read minds.

Just then, Grandmother herself pitter-pats in, deftly balancing a crowded silver dish. 'Little tinker,' she mutters, popping the dish on the table. 'He almost tripped me up.'

Wiping the spit off my chin, I nod understandingly. Then I offer my two pennyworth. 'Crazy critter.'

'So, lemonade then,' she informs me briskly, 'squeezed from my very own lemons. And Fah Sang Pehng.' She nods to a bowl of bronzed buns. 'Your mother told me in her letters how much you enjoy them.'

'I do! I do!' Enthusiastically, I snatch up a

bun. It's still piping hot but I pop it in my mouth anyway. 'Golly! This is superb.' I wink at her and pinch a second, knocking my elbow on the corner of the dish. Flinching, I jerk back my hand, wondering why it hurt so much. 'Even better than Mum's,' I mumble, my teeth clenched in agony.

In truth, her Fah Sang Pehng's not better. To be perfectly honest, Grandmother's buns remind me of dry spaghetti.

I recall Mum baking them for me on my sixteenth birthday, on a wrought-iron tray over a bucket of red hot sand. They'd been so devilishly sweet, full of nuts and with a zesty hint of lemon.

I think she improved considerably on my grandmother's old recipe.

I chew on the insipid bun and watch my grandmother pour. She's only small, perhaps just over four foot, with a bobbly chin, tiny kind eyes and telltale crow's feet. Her nose reminds me of a shrivelled conker and over it a cheeky curl pops out from under her woollen shawl. She has on a cardigan buttoned all the way up to a lacy collar and her slippers look old and scruffy, in need of a bin.

'Did you see much of my garden from up in your tree?' she asks me.

'Yes. Yes, I did. I spotted lots of bamboo trees and orchids.'

She nods. 'If you look, you will see chrysanthemums too,' she says. 'Difficult to spot mind, only tiny blossoms now. Oh, and a plum tree. The Chinese call them all the Junzi flowers. Very hardy. They blossom in the winter, even in the snow.'

She picks up the milk jug.

'Just a drop,' I tell her, rubbing my elbow. It still feels a little tender.

'Your mother wrote to me and told me what happened to Sylva. I'm so terribly sorry.'

I nod a silent thank you.

She hands me a slightly misshaped cup. Her handiwork, I guess. Then she plops down on the sofa next to me. 'I pray for her, you know, and for you.'

I'm reminded of what Colonel Fiquet had told me in the hospital tent in France: 'Hell's the odds on favourite for you, Major...'. Eyes hooded, I look to the old lady. 'Don't bother,' I tell her frankly, 'well, not for me. Sadly, that ship's pulled up anchor and left port.'

Thoughtfully, she sips her lemonade. 'You know, I think I will anyway.'

I nod and sip my lemonade too. Inadvertently, my lips pucker up. Golly, it's bitter.

'I'm so very happy to see you, Tor,' she pats my knee, her crow's feet wrinkling up happily, 'but I hardly think you travelled all the way to China just to enjoy my currant buns.'

Grandmother Toyi may be old, but she's no fool. So, I tell her.

I tell her how I lost my men to the German cannons, had escaped on horseback and ship to Denmark and had been handed the job of stopping the assassination of Karl XV of Sweden. I tell her how Granny Moth, a SWARM assassin, had murdered Gurli, how I had spent twelve months in London trying to find her and how I had been kidnapped off the Flying Spur and taken to this school of ninja.

Grandmother Toyi's eyes now look wider than the rim of the cup on her lap. I think, maybe, I shocked her.

'So this er, Moth-woman; she hurt your cheek?'

'No. The German cannons did.'

She nods sadly and plays for a moment with a button on her cardigan. 'This Hornet Temple is a very dangerous place,' she whispers. 'Why, in September, a boy's body was discovered in the pond up there.'

Dumbstruck, I drop my bun on the floor. Wu's golden dart frogs!

'Murdered, no doubt, but nobody knows who did it. The police hushed it up, you see. The owner, never met him, but they say he's a very powerful fellow.' She drops to a whisper. 'He even knows Empress Cixi and she's a monster.'

I nod knowingly and reluctantly pick up the bun. Yes, she is.

Grandmother sips her lemonade but the cup jitters in her hand and she spills most of it on her cardigan. 'You must run or they will murder you too.'

'I can't,' I tell her sternly. 'SWARM murdered Sylva but they got off scot free. No trial, no prison, no hangman's rope. Nobody's interested in justice for her but me. Just me. If I don't stop them, nobody will.'

'Gurli.'

'Sorry?'

'You told me SWARM murdered Gurli, not

your sister, Sylva.'

'Yes. Yes, I know. Did I...'

'Yes, you did.'

With a thoughtful look, Grandmother pops her cup on the floor by her slippered feet. 'It is not your job to keep everybody in this world safe.'

'She put all her trust in me,' I rub my throbbing temple, 'and I let her down.'

'Who? Gurli or Sylva?'

I look to the Chinese cracker flower and try to find comfort there. So many problems. Mentally, I pop them in a box and shift it to a cobwebby corner in the back of my mind. I pull my botany book from the inner pocket of my tunic and hand it to her. 'Here, let me show you the flowers from my trip.'

She thumbs slowly through it. 'Oh my! This is truly wonderful.' She stops at the picture of the lemon trees. 'You drew them perfectly,' she tells me. 'My grandson is very gifted.'

I remember, a little uncomfortably, that Wu had thought the lemon trees were very good too.

'I see the box of inks I sent to Sweden for your birthday travelled here with you.'

'Yes, they did.' I do not tell her it is still on the Flying Spur and probably lost to me forever.

'I know,' she says with a blossoming smile. 'You must draw my Chinese cracker flower.'

I nod and return her smile. 'I'd enjoy that.'

Grandmother pops the flower pot on the coffee table and hands me a bunch of stubby pencils. 'I hope they will do,' she says.

'Perfectly,' I answer.

'Good. Good.' Then she picks up the stool by the potter's wheel and drops it by my elbow. 'I can see better from here,' she tells me, plonking her bottom on it to watch.

I begin to hunt through my book for a blank page.

'You know, the troops you lost in France, they were not your responsibility.'

'I know.'

'And nor was Gurli or poor little Sylva.'

I swallow and lick the nub of a green pencil. I'm a little nervous. Usually, I only draw when I'm by myself.

'Your Grandpa left this world on June 4th, 1842,' she suddenly blurts out. 'He choked on a hazelnut, the silly old fool. Just over there, by the bookshelf. It took Doctor Chi almost a half

hour to travel here from town. He was busy, you see. A half hour! Your poor Grandpa was bluer than a summer's day by then.'

Absentmindedly, she taps the book. 'Begin with the stem. Green, Tor, not red.'

I scowl. 'Oh yes,' I say slowly. 'Silly me.' Switching pencils, I begin to draw.

'I blamed him, you know, Doctor Chi, and the lady he had been so busy with. Too busy to help my dying husband. She'd been with child, you see and there'd been complications. Later, she had a baby boy. I blamed him too. I remember, years later, when he cycled by my house I threw plums at him. Knocked him off twice. He's thirty now, works in the bakery, but he's still frightened of me.

'This boy, Gripenstedt's son, when your mother told me in her letter you had shot him, I understood why…'

'An eye for an eye,' I murmur nonchalantly.

'No, Tor.' She eyes me sadly. 'Murder is never the answer to murder. I think, perhaps, months, years from now, you will think of Gripenstedt's cowardly boy and no longer feel anger, only sorrow.'

'He killed my sister,' I say testily. 'I can

never feel sorry for him,'.

'Not for him, no,' she puts her hands tidily on her knees, 'but for yourself, for what you did to him.'

Grandmother Toyi picks up the photograph of me off the window sill and looks at it. 'I can hardly see any of this innocent boy in the cavalry major here today.'

I chuckle. 'I was only six. This fellow, Mr Blomqvist I think, took it in Sunday school. He had the only camera in the north of Sweden. I had just been to church in Jokkmokk and I had on this crazy Hawaiian shirt Father had picked up for me on his trip to the island.' I think for a moment, lost in the old memory. 'I remember the vicar had not been too happy. He thought it not at all proper for church.'

'But look how skinny you were,' she hands me the photograph, 'and look at you now. A bull of a man.'

I look to the smiling boy and smile back. 'I did fill out.'

'In your mother's letters to me, she described how green your eyes were, with a hint of grey. You had her eyes she told me, eyes she inherited from me. But now I see there's a spot

of yellow in them too, just by the pupils.' She chews thoughtfully on her lip. 'How odd.'

There had been no mirror on the Flying Spur and there's no mirror in my room in Hornet Temple, so this is news to me. Or is it? On the Gulong, Yi's ship, did I not see my eyes reflected in the sword's steel, burning yellow? What is happening to me, I wonder. My temper is almost uncontrollable and I fancy chopping up Grandmother's cat and enjoying it sushi-style.

Or in a crumble.

Or soup. Yes. Yes! Soup. Cat soup with lots and lots of croutons and...

Hastily, I drop the photo on her lap and turn my eyes back to the safety of the Chinese cracker flower. 'The stem is very difficult to draw,' I tell her. 'So many thorns.'

'What's bothering you, Tor?'

With a reluctant sigh, I look up from my sketch book. 'I wish I knew, Grandmother,' I tell her. 'But whatever it is, it's in me. It torments me, plays with me and fills me with a terrible fury.' I toss the book on the coffee table, almost upsetting the flower pot. 'I'm just a puppet and a demon's my puppeteer.'

Gently, she cups my hand in hers. 'If there truly is a demon in you,' she prods my chest, 'in here, then he'll not be there for ever. Remember Tor, it is a man's own mind, not his enemy's, who tempts him to evil ways.' Her tiny smile brightens the room. 'You must show this demon who's boss.'

I attempt to match her smile but a shadow envelops my lips and darkens my words. Slowly, my eyes flutter shut. 'I can see him now, hidden in the very corner of my mind, in my blood, hungry for...'

I feel her grip stiffen. 'For what, Tor?'

My eyes blink open as if I'd just opened the door on a sunny day. For a moment, I'm tempted to say her cat. 'I don't know, Grandmother,' I murmur. I suddenly feel worn out and desperately in need of sleep. 'But I do know this, every day he grows stronger and he's tired of hiding.'

Thursday, 4th February, 1872
Assassination Day

0212 hours, Yixin's Castle, Wuxi

I squeeze my foot in a tiny chink in the rock and lever my aching body up the cliff. Almost to the top now, I determinedly keep my eyes on the rock face and not on the two hundred and fifty foot drop to the ebony waters of Tai Hu Lake. It is difficult work but the row of metal studs on my palms help a lot and my ninja boots, laced up like ladders to my shins, seem almost possessed, magically finding every nook and tiny cranny for my poor befuddled feet.

My climb is not helped by the bow and the quiver of arrows on my back and the two wooden barrels and paddle slung over my shoulder. They mercilessly sand my skin red-raw.

Thankfully, the welts I expected to see on my chest from my run in with Grandmother's cat did not blossom. What did blossom was a red blotch on my elbow just where it struck my grandmother's silver tray.

Very odd. Very odd indeed.

With every muscle in my body yelling at me to stop, I finally drag myself over the lip of the cliff. There, I rest for a moment to recover my strength.

With a little help from the quarter moon, I

quickly spot the towers of Yixin's castle. It is only sixty odd yards away but there is hardly any cover between it and me. Thankfully, my black ninja uniform keeps me well camouflaged and I creep over to the castle's murky-looking moat without being seen.

I spot a deer lapping on a muddy puddle. With a scowl, I wonder why she prefers to drink from there and not the moat. I hunt in my pocket for tsune no mizu, a ninja food of pickled plums and diced pork, and toss it in the water.

Volcanically, the water churns up and I'm left with a very scary answer.

PIRANHA!

Thankfully, I had thought of this, well, Wu had, and I'm prepared.

The mizugumo or water spider is a very clever ninja tool for crossing water and not getting wet. Or eaten! I unhook the two barrels off my back and slip my feet in them. Then, with the help of the paddle, I begin to walk Jesus-like over to the far bank.

I'm a little wobbly in my bobbing barrels and twice I almost topple in, plunging my hand for just a split second in the tepid water. Instantly,

I feel the teeth of the piranha on my finger tips and when I pull my hand away, the dripping blood sends the fish into a wild frenzy.

But I keep my nerve and by very gently dipping my paddle into the frothing water, I make it across. I then hide the barrels under a handy thorn bush. I will need them on my return trip.

If there is a return trip.

A twig snaps and I drop low, my eyes scanning the distant bank. I spot the deer is still there. I swallow and turn my back on it. I almost wet my ninja uniform.

I can see Yixin's castle properly now, a labyrinth of shadowy roofs and blackened windows. It is on a low hill surrounded by a wall. A handy cloud blankets the moon and I sprint the twenty feet over to it.

I unwind a rope and grappling hook from my body, then, keeping a firm grip on the end, I toss the hook up and over the towering wall. I pull it and it holds. Then, hand over hand, foot over foot, I scramble up it.

Once on the top, I rest. Wu told me how important it is for a ninja to stop, look and most importantly, think. So, I perch on top of the wall and do just that. I quickly spy the back door to the castle and by the slim trunk of a rubber tree, a sleeping sentry. I watch his chest, my eyes narrowing. I can tell he's only snoozing. I must find a way to help him to sleep a little deeper.

Silently, I slip a stumpy bamboo shoot from my sleeve pocket. It's the ninja blowpipe, effective up to thirty feet, the dart in it tipped with a tiny drop of henbane sap. I put the tip of the bamboo to my lips and blow sharply, the dart hitting the sentry squarely on the cheek.

Probably thinking it's a mosquito, he flaps a lazy hand at his face, dislodging the dart. It drops on his lap, but I need not worry. The henbane is already pumping through his body and a split second later his chin drops back to his chest. He'll now sleep deeply for twelve hours.

I urgently pull up the rope, anchor it and drop silently to the freshly-cut lawn.

Ever so softly, I creep over to the snoring sentry. The moon is still in a helpful mood and shows me a key on his belt. Gingerly, I drop to my knees and unhook it, the potent smell of rice wine lingering in my nostrils. Alcohol - and

henbane sap! He will sleep well. I step over him to the door and with a hasty prayer, I slip the key in the lock. Twisting it, there is a satisfying clunk.

Pulling the door ajar, my gaze is met by a gloomy corridor. I instantly remember what Empress Cixi had told me in the Forbidden City, '...there will be a number of clever and very nasty booby traps.'

I need a light.

I hurry over to the rubber tree I had seen from the top of the wall and peel off a chunk of bark. Under it, it is slimy and sticky. I rip off the cuff of my sleeve and dip it in the goo, then I pull the bamboo blowpipe out of my pocket and wrap the sticky cloth around the tip. I light it with a match.

For a second or so I eye the dancing flame. I'm no longer clumsy and, it seems, I'm no longer allergic to cats. Why, then, when I now see fire do I tremble in my boots?

Squaring my shoulders, I begin to shuffle my way down the corridor. Unfortunately, the floor is pebbly and my feet crunch a booming 'HELLO! HERE I AM!' to any lurking enemy. The torch in my hand boldly combats the shadows, but in truth, there is not much to see, only cracked walls and cobwebby corners.

Abruptly, the floor in front of me drops away and I stop. There is a low buzzing and I wonder nervously what is making it.

Reluctantly, I drop to my knees to get a better look. There is a hole, perhaps six feet deep and six feet wide, completely filling the corridor. In the bottom of it I spot what looks to be a football. Sadly however, it is not. It is, in fact, a hornets' nest.

Admittedly a clever trap in a horrifically evil sort of way, the blind intruder tumbling in there and landing on it.

The Chinese hornet is not a particularly happy fellow and the sting of twenty of them can kill a baby elephant. The thought of being trapped in there with a few hundred of them...

I shudder at the thought.

The trap is only ten, maybe eleven feet end to end, no problem for me now. I sprint up to it and jump, my knees tucked up to my chin. I hit the floor perfectly, so perfectly I wonder for a second if I'd been adopted and my actual parents were circus acrobats.

My torch, I see, is no longer lit, but I still see

perfectly. With a chuckle, I drop the blowpipe on the tunnel floor. I do not need it. I forgot, with my new powers, I can now see perfectly in the dark.

I plough on, and turning a sharp corner I find myself in a room wall to wall with towering plants. In fact, it is so crowded with creepers and the yellow-petalled rose it will be difficult to squeeze by them all.

I wonder how this could possibly be a trap. I shuffle over to a bush and tentatively sniff the flower. It smells wonderful, if not ever so slightly acidic. With a thoughtful tut, I step back and from under my boot there is a soft pop.

Pulling my foot instinctively up, I drop to a knee and discover a very squashed frog. I scratch my brow thoughtfully, the wheels in my skull slowly picking up speed. The skin is scaly, crusty-looking, the eyes red - well, I think so anyway; it is difficult to tell. They popped when I trod on it.

I remember the golden dart frogs in Wu's pond; that he had put in the Emperor's silk pyjamas. I also remember his words, 'The venom in the skin will kill a rhino.'

With stampeding elephants in my belly, I peer under the flowers. Blimey! There must be hundreds of them. Then the penny drops. With so many frogs, the dirt will be laced with venom and so will the plants growing in it.

Hopping to my feet, I look back to the flower I had just smelt and the thorn under it. The tip, I see, is yellow and sappy.

I must find a way to slip by them, but if a thorn pricks my skin, I know I will be almost instantly killed.

Gritting my teeth, I begin to slowly squeeze my way by the flowers. Every vine is carpeted with thorns and I must twist and bend to keep them from ripping the thin cloth of my ninja uniform. My feet order me to run, to bulldoze my way out of there, but my mind tells them sternly to, 'SHUT UP!' and not to do anything silly.

I keep my wits and wiggle my way on. Eventually, the rows of flowers stop. I stop too and wipe my dripping brow. Killer fish, killer bees and now, killer flowers. What next, I wonder. Killer kittens? A warren of killer bunny rabbits?

The corridor winds endlessly on, until,

finally, I turn a sharp corner and there I see an archway and the moon sitting low in the sky. I drop to my belly and crawl up to what I hope is the exit.

Warily, I peer out.

I see a courtyard, and there, in the very middle of it, a temple. It looks very, very old, all curvy and sleepy, perhaps in need of a cup of hot milk and a sleep. On the steps up to the temple I spot a number of troops. I count twenty of them. Too many even for me. Yixin must be in there. If not, why the troops?

My eyes hunt the lanterned courtyard and almost instantly I spot my target. A stable in a far off corner. The roof, I see, is thatched. Quickly, I unhook the bow from my shoulder and pull a straw-tipped arrow from the quiver on my back.

I set a match to it.

Trying to keep my eye on the stable and off the dancing flame, I fit the butt of the arrow to the string and let fly.

BULLSEYE! But then, I can hit a plum from a hundred feet.

A second later, the roof erupts.

'FIRE!' yells a sentry, jumping to his feet and

all but the oldest of them hurry over to the stable.

With the lightning speed of a cheetah, I sprint up the steps. Luckily, the trooper is busy cheering on his firefighting pals and his back is to me. Luckily for me, not for him. I stop and cheekily tap him on the shoulder with my bow.

Instantly, he twirls on his heels and his fists fly up. But I keep my wits and throw a pocketful of sawdust in his eyes, momentarily blinding him. The sharp ends of my bow hammer his chin and soft belly and in a blaze of thumps, I knock him cold.

Hooking the bow back over my shoulder, I hurry up the steps to Yixin's temple. Undoubtedly, the rest of his troops will soon be back so I sprinkle caltrops on the top of the steps to slow them up a little. Then, I pull my trusty sword, Tyrfing, mentally cross my fingers, and slither open the door.

'So, my wonderful sister, Cixi, finally sent her killer.'

A chunky man in a floppy-sleeved silk kimono is stood in the room. He is perhaps only twenty or so but he has the beefy shoulders of an overworked smithy and the thoughtful eyes

of a storyteller. A perfectly trimmed moustache hovers over his top lip, but it looks sort of stupid. He is too young for such a 'pipe and slippers' look.

I watch him march over to me, a panther on the hunt, his beefy legs swirling up his robe and the sword on his belt. He looks madder than a rabid dog.

In a flash, he pulls his blade.

'NO!' I howl, but he is on me in the blink of an eye.

Our swords hit in a blaze of steel and a flurry of powdery sparks. I remember Cixi told me he's a very accomplished swordsman, and he is. Excellent, in fact. He attacks and I try to parry but with a wild cry he jumps six feet off the floor, twirls and with a twist of his wrist rips my uniform from rib to belly button.

Grumpily, I finger the torn cloth.

'Yixin, I'm not here to...' But he cuts off my words by dropping to his knee and stabbing me brutally in the ankle.

He hops to his feet, his sword up.

'LOOK HERE!' I explode, waggling my foot at him. 'Now my boot's torn too. I only got them on Wednesday.'

With cold eyes, I parry his next attack, spin and stop my blade a whisker from his cheek. I battle not only him but to keep my temper in check. If I kill him my plan is doomed. I think of the Junzi flowers: the curvy splendour of the orchid, the soft thump of the dropping plum, the knock, knock, knock of the bamboo in the wind...

'*Kill the pig,*' the demon growls in my skull.

'No,' the angel begs me. '*He will help us to destroy SWARM.*'

The softer words win the day and, little by little, the fury in my chest drops to a simmer; a pot of bubbling water snatched off the hob.

With the tip of my sword still tickling Yixi's cheek, he back-pedals, only to trip over a stool and thump to the floor.

'GUARDS!' he bellows. Instantly his troops storm in. Many of them seem to be limping: my caltrops did the trick.

I press my sword to his chest. 'Yixin, my name is Major Tor and Cixi did send me to murder you...'

His eyes shimmer with fury.

'...but don't worry. I won't hurt you. I only wish to talk to you.'

'So you can tell me how you plan to murder me,' he rages.

'No.' I pull my sword from his cheek. 'So I can tell you how to destroy Empress Cixi, your psychopathic sister-in-law.'

He eyes me doubtfully, but allows me to pull him to his feet. I can tell by the knot of his eyebrows he's wondering if he can trust me or not. Then he nods to his troops and they scurry from the room.

A verdict in my favour.

'There's a school of ninjas in Ningpo run by a chap called Wu Tong,' I tell him. 'Your sister instructed Wu to murder you and he handed me the job.'

Yixin's shoulders droop and he drops dejectedly to the stool he had tripped over. 'I know of this Hornet Temple. Cixi has a spy there but he happens to be my spy too. That is how I knew of your trip to the Forbidden City.'

'Then it was your men who attacked our ship; Cixi thought so.'

'Yes. Good men too; loyal. A pity you and this Wu-fellow killed them.'

'Your men's swords were just as sharp as ours,' I tell him frostily.

He grunts but slowly nods.

Determinedly, I carry on with my story. 'Wu works for SWARM, a secret organisation of assassins based in London. I plan to destroy them, but to do it, you must vanish for three weeks. Your men must tell the world you were murdered in your sleep. They must even bury you,' I wink mischievously, 'or pretend to anyway.

'Then, three weeks from today, you can tell the people of China how Cixi attempted to murder you, her only brother, but did not succeed. Her cowardly act will hurt her. Her popularity will suffer and you will be the hero of the hour.' I smile wickedly. 'She'll be terribly upset.'

'Works for me,' murmurs Yixin, with a mirroring smile. 'But if I know my beloved sister-in-law, feet will be chopped off.'

I nod, remembering what a monster she is. 'She'll think SWARM betrayed her. She'll order her General Li to destroy Hornet Temple and with no ninja schools in China, you will be considerably safer.'

Yixin chews thoughtfully on his lip. 'These three weeks seem very important to you, Major.

Why is that?' He eyes me sullenly. 'Why can I not tell the world of Cixi's treachery now? Today?'

'If SWARM thinks I did my job and killed you, they will trust me. I will be Genin, a ninja agent. I will be told SWARM's secrets and sent to London to work. There, I can destroy them.

'If you keep low for the three weeks, when Wu finally discovers I didn't murder you, I will be half way to England and no ship will be able to catch me. I will have ample time to infiltrate SWARM's HQ in London before Wu can send word of my betrayal.'

I put my hand gently on his shoulder. 'I understand if destroying SWARM is not top of your 'to do' list, but know this, they murdered your brother, the emperor, and Cixi ordered them to do it.'

Yixi springs to his feet. 'WITCH!' he bellows. 'My brother loved her; the silly fool even trusted her. Is nobody safe from her claws?' He begins to pace the room, his temple throbbing. 'I will, I will - rip off her...'

I hush his angry blusterings with the urgent snap of my fingers. A putrid stench just drifted up my nostrils. I scowl and sniff. Rotten fish and, and...

OLD SMELLY BOOTS!

'I told Mr Spider not to trust you.' The hissed words spill over me. I look up to the temple roof and to my horror I spot a man crouched on a rafter, his face lost in shadow to a black hood.

But I know who it is. I know his stink.

BEE!

The assassin thumps to the floor. 'I bet Wu didn't tell you I'd be your back up on this job.'

'No,' I utter, my eyes cemented to the shimmering tip of his sword. 'Probably slipped his mind.'

I had been wrong then to blame the deer for snapping the twig. It must have been Bee. The clownish thug has been on my heels every step of the way.

'GUARDS!' yells Yixin for the second time.

A dozen of his troops hurry in but in a flurry of steel Bee cuts them to ribbons. I chew on my lip, tasting blood. Bee's a very skilled swordsman.

With a jackal's howl, Yixin pulls his own sword.

'NO!' I cry. 'HE WILL KILL YOU!' But his

anger blocks my words and he attacks. The clown ducks and rolls and with a swipe of his sword sends Yixin tumbling. Cixi's brother-in-law hits the wall, his body lost in a jumble of splintered wood.

The ninja drops his blade to the floor and pulls off his hood. 'No swift sword in the belly for you, Tor,' he growls, drawing his brow together into a merciless scowl. 'I want to feel every bone in your body shatter in my hands.'

I swallow, remembering the poor dummy's wooden chest. Then, reluctantly, I too drop my sword.

He lumbers over to me, his fists flying but I can also duck and roll. With a jackal's cry, he jumps up, his foot shooting for my chin but I block it perfectly and thump him in the belly with the heel of my hand. He staggers back, hitting the wall, a string of profanity spilling with the drool from his lips. Quickly, I snatch up the stool, rip off a leg and tomahawk it across the room. It hits him squarely between the eyebrows. I storm up to him, drop low and sweep my foot, but he skips nimbly over it. Then, with blood flooding his eyes, he's on me. I hop up and thump him; an uppercut to the chin. Then I twist and flip him over my shoulder, cartwheeling him to the floor. Snorting and puffing like an enraged bull, he clambers drunkenly to his feet but, calmly, my boot pulps his knee and I watch him topple over onto his bottom.

Stunned and numb with horror, he looks up at me. 'Even Mr Spider is no match for you,' he whimpers.

I grin. 'That's very good news,' I tell him matter-of-factly.

Then, magically, he pulls a tiny pistol from his sleeve and levels it at my chest.

I feel my stomach lurch but I do not step back. 'Wu told me ninja prefer bows and arrows,' I say calmly.

'They do,' he admits, his words thick and muffled on his swollen lips. He clambers drunkenly to his feet. 'But I think it's important to have the odd trick up my sleeve. Literally.'

I swallow. 'So I see.'

'Anyway,' the clown sneers, 'a bow won't fit up there.'

BOOM! He is only a foot away and cannot miss. But I see the bullet. I CAN ACTUALLY SEE IT! It's as if it's hopped up on a slow ball

and I catch it perfectly in my hand.

The volcano in me erupts, vomiting red hot lava over any thoughts of Junzi flowers or angelic words. I drop swiftly to my knee, the heel of my other hand hammering Bee's chest. A cannon ball hitting a papery wall. He thumps to the floor, a tiny drop of blood dribbling from the corner of his lips and down over his cheek.

His eyelids flutter. He is dying but ruthlessly I turn away. I have seen it happen to much better men.

I sprint over to the limp body of Yixin and pull the splintered wood off him. 'Do you need a doctor?' I cry urgently.

'No, no.' With an anguished grunt, he sits up. 'He just scratched me. I hit my brow too; knocked me silly.'

I nod. Thankfully, he seems almost unhurt, just a bump over his eye and a tiny cut to his belly under the ribs. 'I know Cixi will only destroy Hornet Temple and the school if she thinks SWARM botched the job and did not murder her husband's brother. It seems my plan is still intact.

Yixin eyes me warily. 'I remember when I was just a boy, my father, the emperor, took me and my elder brother to the zoo. The keepers showed us a wolf but he was sleeping. So they put a sheep in with him; they wanted the wolf to put on a good show for the important visitors.

'You remind me of that wolf, your speed, the way you brawl and scrap. The ninja over there was just a sheep to you.' His frown deepens. 'But I must tell you, Major, even a wolf can't catch a bullet.'

I pull him to his feet. 'The man was half blind,' I tell him blithely. 'He'd find it difficult to shoot a caged elephant.'

But there's truth to his words. I remember how the Icelandic wolf, Skufsi Tennur, had bitten me, and how, within seconds, I'd felt so very powerful. Is it possible...

I mentally kick myself; now is not the moment to brood over this. I must try to keep my mind on my job.

'Don't forget, Yixin,' I sternly say, discreetly dropping the bullet through a crack in the wooden floor, 'you must keep low for three weeks. If SWARM discovers I betrayed them too soon, I will never stop them.'

He nods and puts his hand on my shoulder. 'I

wonder, Major Tor, why it is you do this crazy job. Nobody's paying you to stop SWARM,' his eyes narrow, 'or perhaps there is.'

'No, nobody's paying me.' I swallow and smile jadedly. 'They murdered a little girl,' I tell him simply, 'and her dreams.'

Slowly, I hobble over to my sword and pick it up. I feel spent; the cut on my foot throbs mercilessly and sleep tempts my eyelids. I just want to curl up in a ball and drift off to a better world.

If a better world exists...

'He had your yellow eyes too.'

I scowl and I feel my stomach scrunch up. 'Sorry?'

'The wolf. In the zoo.'

For a thoughtful second I thumb the ruby in Tyrfing's hilt. I'm remembering who also had yellow eyes. Miss Butterfly and, and...I frown, trying to recall.

A sentry on the floor whimpers and the spell is broken.

I snap off a bow and turn to the door. Now I must return to Hornet Temple. Now I must fool Wu.

Saturday, 6th February, 1872
72 Days to Assassination Day

0710 hours, Hornet Temple

Once more I'm back in the Rimankya Room. It is packed wall to wall with Wu's students and the ninja who school them in the tricky art of murder. Wu is stood next to me and next to him a poker rests ominously in a bucket of red hot embers.

'Students of Hornet Temple, today we welcome Major Tor, from here on to be called Mr Locust, to the ranks of SWARM.' Wu looks to me, his eyes deathly cold. 'Genin ninja, you may now call me Mr Wasp.'

I swallow and try to look indifferent to this mammoth news; difficult with my eyebrows climbing so swiftly up my brow. So this is Wasp, the brother of Grasshopper, who had attacked me and who I had killed on the Flying Spur.

If anybody ever tells him...

'To begin with, Major, you must recite SWARM's oath of allegiance.' He hands me a scroll. 'Try not to whisper,' he says stonily.

'This room is very big. Oh, and er, from the soul, yes?'

I nod. Do assassins have souls, I wonder, unrolling the parchment and studying the words. Then, a little reluctantly, I begin. 'I will uphold the honour of the ninja, follow Mr Spider's orders and keep the secrets of SWARM, the Sepulchre of World Assassins, Ransomers and Mutineers, from all who wish to destroy it.'

There is a muted cheer and everybody claps. Sort of. Just for a second or two. I don't think they trust me. Clever kids.

With the flamboyancy of a circus clown, Wu pulls the poker from the fire. On the tip of it I spy a red hot lump of iron in the shape of a spider. I clench my teeth. HE PLANS TO BRAND MY WRIST!

I watch him stroll over to me, embers of joy dancing in his devilish eyes.

'This may sting just a little,' he chirrups optimistically.

I swallow, the thought of the red hot stamp on my skin terrifying me. I try to back away but all too soon my bottom hits the tapestry draped wall. 'You know, I don't mind if you just tattoo it on.' My words rising to a hysterical whine.

'Major! Major!' He titters pitilessly. 'There'd be no fun in that.'

'But...'

He cuts me off by snatching my hand, twisting it and stamping the iron to my tender skin.

My knees buckle and with a cry, I sink pathetically to the floor. There, I promptly throw up over Wu's feet.

The ninja looks on, a smirk playing at the corner of his lips. He's not upset. In fact, I think he thinks he's just discovered my Goyo-Goyuko. FIRE! Unfortunately, I think he's spot on.

'Welcome to SWARM, Mr Locust,' he says triumphantly.

0835 hours

Almost comradely, Wu and I stroll by the flower beds behind Hornet Temple. Summer is in the air now, although the sun is hidden, mopped up by a dishcloth of plump fluffy

clouds. A dry breeze is swirling up my black robe, mercilessly tickling the buds of a baby corn lily. I remember this particularly toxic flower from ninja school. Pop it in your enemy's beef stew and he'll spend the next week or so on the loo. Not the most romantic of flowers to present to your wife on her birthday but, still, very pretty.

I stop and tenderly I stroke the top of a yellow petal with my thumb. Well, I think it's yellow. Everything I see now, even the petals on the flowers, look dirty grey as if the rain has washed away the colour.

I spotted my new handicap when I had mixed up the red and green pencils while trying to draw my grandmother's Chinese cracker flower. I can jump ponds, yes, and I can catch a flying bullet with my hand, but it seems I must pay a price for my new powers. I can no longer see the golden yellows and vibrant reds; I can no longer enjoy the flowers I love so much.

But, thankfully, I can still smell them. The sugar-sweet scent of the plum, the almost overpowering, sneeze-provoking perfume of the lily; I have the nose of a blood hound.

Yes, by God, I can smell them.

I think perhaps I will miss China. Not Wu, his ninja school or his warped philosophy on immorality, and definitely not my daily plate of beef and rice, but I will miss the Chinese cracker flower I can see from my window and my visits to Grandmother Toyi. Perched in my tree, watching her tend to her orchids and chrysanthemums had helped me to stay sane in this topsy-turvy world of depravity and murder.

Yes, her I will miss the most.

I look up from the flower to see Wu eyeing me thoughtfully. 'You know, your old chum, Mr Bee, insisted you'd betray us.' With troubled eyes, Wu rubs his chin and I can tell he feels uncomfortable. 'And I must admit, I had my doubts too, which is why I sent him on the Yixin job to, er...

'Check up on me,' I volunteer helpfully.

'Help you.'

'Oh.' I smile bemusedly. 'I see.'

'But you pulled it off and now my ninja school is safe for the next century. If Cixi keeps her word,' he adds ruefully. Grimly, his eyes cut to his feet. 'When Yixin's men jumped us on the trip to the Forbidden City, you saved my life.' He swallows, the words perhaps jammed

in his larynx. 'Thank you, Tor. '

He looks up, his eyes challenging, daring me to laugh at him.

I don't. 'No problem,' I say.

He nods, his face softening. 'Remember I told you I'd never trust you, well, I do now, just a little mind, but I do. On Shikoku, my island in Japan, they call it kyoudaibun or brotherhood.'

It is ironic. I just spent three months in China; the result, I now know an awful lot of Japanese words.

Embarrassed for him, we wander by the Chinese cracker flower and I stop to smell the buds. They still remind me of tiny, half-peeled bananas.

'So Mr Bee fell on his own sword, you say.'

'Yes. A tragic loss.' I do not even bat my eyelids but resort to rubbing absentmindedly on my spider-shaped burn. Holy cow, it stings. 'Tripped over his boot lace,' I tell him offhandedly. 'Very sloppy of him.'

Wu chews doubtfully on his lip. 'Indeed.'

I decide to steer our little chat out of these shark-infested waters. 'So, now if I commit murder,' I say casually, 'SWARM will pay me to do it. How kind of them.'

Wu grinds his teeth and tuts. He's known me for three months but my tomfoolery still annoys him. 'Now you will be sent to London, Major, sorry, Mr Locust. Old habits. There you will meet the boss of SWARM, my boss, Mr Spider. He will instruct you on your first, no, no, second job. Do try to keep in mind he is not the most tolerant of men.'

'I will do my best.'

He sighs. 'Undoubtedly.'

I shoot him my most beguiling smile. 'Now I'm Genin and a member of SWARM, perhaps you can tell me a few of Mr Spider's dirty little secrets.'

'Hmm.' He chews thoughtfully on his top lip. 'Perhaps.'

He drops to his bottom. The lawn, I see, is still wet with dew but, reluctantly, I sit too.

'SWARM is almost a century old,' he begins. 'In 1792, we murdered King Gustav III of your country, Sweden. A knife to the belly. Very nasty. Then, in 1861, the Xianfeng Emperor,' he smirks, 'my handiwork. On April 15th 1865 we shot US president Abraham Lincoln. A fellow by the name of Booth did the job. John Booth.

We called him Mr Hornet. I schooled him myself.'

'So Hornet Temple...'

'Is named after him, yes. Well, he did do a marvellous job.

'Old supporters of the American confederacy bankrolled the assassination. They were a bit upset, you see, when they lost the civil war. But SWARM soon cheered them up. They even presented us with an ironclad ship, the Alabama, but we call her the Goyo-Goyuku.

'SWARM's philosophy is simple yet very effective. We not only school our students in the skills of the ninja but also in the modern technology of the day. Of tomorrow, if we can.'

I remember the assassin's powerful rifle in Stockholm, the pistol hidden cleverly up Bee's sleeve and the speed of Gulong, the ship we went to the Forbidden City on. Slowly, I nod.

'You say, 'we'...'

'Oh yes, Mr Locust, there is not just this school. There is also a school in Brazil, Mexico, Scotland and Papua New Guinea. Soon there will even be a school in New York, in the US.

'Our HQ is in London, you will soon see where. There, you will meet Mr Spider and his

Circle of Assassins. You may also bump into my brother, Mr Grasshopper. He's over in London on a job. Say hello from me.'

I rally up my most innocent of looks. 'Yes, yes, no problem.' But I very much doubt I will considering he's in the English Channel with a swordfish in his chest and fish nibbling on his eyeballs.

I scratch my cheek and in an off-hand sort of way ask, 'So, this Mr Spider-fellow, who is he? The son of a chimney sweep? Did he murder the milkman and run off to the circus...'

'His identity is top secret,' the ninja interrupts my banter. 'Not even I know who he really is. But there is a rumour, only a rumour mind, he's a confidant of Queen Victoria.' Assuming a mysterious face, he winks conspiringly.

'Remember Mr Locust, follow Mr Spider's orders to the letter, to the full stop if you must. There's no room in SWARM for democracy. Our boss is, for want of a better word, or, perhaps not, a dictator. He will not suffer fools. Carry out his commands or suffer.'

I remember the words of the assassin who had played the role of Duke Solbakken so well.

'Spider is not born of Eve,' he had wheezed, the blowfish venom savaging his organs. Was the boss of SWARM not even human then?

I choose my next words circumspectly. 'It is, don't you think, a very odd profession to be in. Murder. No cycle to work, no up with the cockerel.'

'I'm an assassin,' Wu tells me sternly, 'not a murderer.'

I hastily nod. 'Sorry,' I mumble. I don't want to upset the man; not now he's opening up. 'But how do you sleep, you know, when tomorrow you must slip blowfish blood in a punchbowl or a golden dart frog in the emperor's silk pyjamas?'

'I sleep like a baby,' he tells me stonily.

'A baby tends to wake up every three hours and cry,' I retort.

He eyeballs me, the corner of his lips twitching up. I think he is trying to smile but, perhaps, he's forgotten how to. 'Then I must wake up every three hours and cry,' he says.

I swallow. This ninja really is colder than a block of ice. 'But why do it?' I persist. 'I really want to know.'

He blows out his cheeks, then. 'I can only

speculate on such things, but I think Mr Spider, for all his talk of world order, simply enjoys the power. Granny Moth, however, is a lady of luxury. She's in it to fill her coffers. And myself,' he shrugs, 'for me it is just a job; the path I happen to travel on. My Uncle Yi, you met him, he's the skipper of the Gulong, the ship we went to the Forbidden City on. My sister, Soo Po, you met her too, is a trusted member of Cixi's inner circle. And I, well, I just happen to be a professional assassin.'

I look to him in reluctant awe. It seems Yi and Soo Po were born in Japan too and not China. No wonder the lady in the Forbidden City, Wu's sister it now seems, had spoken Japanese so well. It is difficult not to admire the audacity of this man. Every member of his family works for him or is a spy for him.

Wu rubs thoughtfully on his chin. Shifting my wet bottom, I wonder, a little nervously, what is on his mind.

'So, Mr Locust, you're now a fully pledged ninja. A Genin spy, no less.' He eyes me sceptically. 'In just over, what, three months of study? Truly a miracle considering it took me ten years.'

I widen my eyes innocently. 'The school I went to was excellent.'

Irritably, he flaps his hand, dismissing my modesty. 'And not just any old ninja, but most probably the finest in Hornet Temple history, perhaps in the history of any of SWARM's schools.'

'But for you, Sensei.'

'Hmm, perhaps.' His lips curl up depreciatingly. He enjoys being petted; if he was a cat, he'd purr. 'I see power in you, Mr Locust, and it is not just the power of man. Or of a ninja. I do not pretend to fully comprehend it, but, if I may, I can offer you a few words of advice.'

He eyes me, almost warily, and I nod for him to carry on.

'You must channel this - whatever it is, control it if you can, or it will control you. But most importantly, never allow it to choose the target for your blade.'

I remember he had told me this in the Rimankya Room the day he had almost murdered me. Had he known of my powers even then?

'Thank you for your thoughtful words,' I tell

him with a respectful bob of my head. 'I will think on them on my journey to London.'

My mind is in a whirl but I cannot risk showing it. Not to Wu anyway. It may seem he is trying to help me, but I do not trust this man. He knows I'm scared stiff of fire and now he is just probing for my second Goyo-Goyuko. A second way to hurt me. I think deep, deep down he knows I'm truly still his enemy.

But I know his Goyo-Goyuko too. The all-powerful and totally unpredictable Empress Cixi. Oh, and his second. The fool drinks too much.

Suddenly, I remember what bothered on my trip to China. 'Tell me, Mr, er - Wasp. why is it SWARM attempted to murder everybody at the party in Stockholm and not just the Swedish king?'

Wu thinks for a moment, then, slowly, he says, 'To be perfectly honest, Mr Locust, I do not know.'

I watch my tutor unfold his limbs and hop athletically to his feet. 'Now all there is for me to do is to wish you favourable winds.' His grins crookedly. 'And God help anybody who attempts to cross you.'

His eyes flicker momentarily to the pond. 'You never did jump it.'

'No,' I spring up too and squarely meet his gaze, 'I never did.'

Saturday, 4th March, 1872
44 Days to Assassination Day

1020 hours, Hornet Temple

'WU! WU!'

Soo Po runs into the Rimankya Room where her brother is demonstrating to his class of students the Japanese art of Bojitsu, or stick fighting.

The ninja looks up and scowls. His sister is his most valuable spy in the Forbidden City. If Cixi has a spy in Hornet Temple, he will now tell the empress of Soo Po's betrayal.

His sister scampers up to him and bows. 'Yixin, Cixi's brother, just arrived in Beijing. There's not a scratch on him.'

Wu's chin slumps to his chest. 'That's not possible,' he rasps.

'Major Tor did not complete his mission. It

seems he only killed Mr Bee and now Cixi knows and she's mad.' She chews frantically on her top lip. 'She sent General Li and his troops to murder you and to burn down your school.'

Wu's students gasp and a babble of excited whispers erupt in the room.

'But Major Tor told me...'

'He tricked you, Brother.' She grips his elbow. 'It took me a week to travel here. Cixi's army is on my heels. They will be here any second.'

The Japanese ninja looks out on the crowd of boys, his mind in a whirl. But he's determined not to show it. He needs them to defend the school so he can flee the coop. 'It is your duty to protect Hornet Temple,' he instructs them coldly. 'Do not let Cixi's troops destroy it.'

They hurry over to the door, overly keen to meet the swords of the Chinese troops. Or, perhaps, they had mistaken Wu's words and they think he yelled, 'HOLIDAYS!'

Wu twirls on his heels and his eyes meet Soo Po's. 'Ride to the Grand Canal in Wuxi,' he tells her sternly. 'Uncle Yi is there, Qin too. All of you must return to Japan.'

'But Wu, I can't just...'

Harshly, her older brother cuts her off. 'Many months ago, a boy was murdered in the gardens here. I suspect Cixi has a spy in Hornet Temple, probably a student, and I think he did it. Why, I do not know. If he's spotted you and undoubtedly he has, he will report your betrayal to her.' He puts his hand on her shoulder. 'If she finds you, she will chop off your feet.'

'Come with us then.'

'Soo Po, you know I can never return to Japan. Anyway,' he sighs majestically, 'I'm needed in London. Mr Spider will need my help to stop Major Tor.'

A slow-burning frown knots Soo Po's brow. 'But Mr Spider's skilled in Kong fu. Can he not stop Tor by himself?'

'No, he cannot.' Wu thumps the wall with his fist, splintering the wood. 'The major is not simply a ninja, he's a very gifted killer and he just spent three months in Hornet Temple sharpening his sword.'

Wu pulls his sister to his chest and hugs her. 'Goodbye Soo Po. Everything I do - did, was for the family. Try to think kindly of me.'

'Goodbye brother. I love you.' She pulls away. 'You love me too, don't you?'

'Yes. Yes, I do.'

Watching her scurry away, Wu feels his spirits slump. They had had a difficult childhood, forced to flee Japan, the country they loved, but still he worships his family: his brother, his sister, his Uncle Yi and his nephew, Qin. He will miss them terribly. Then his spirits lift. Perhaps he will see his younger brother, Mr Grasshopper, in London.

There is an echoing boom and the north wall of the room blows up in a tempest of flying splinters.

Cannons!

Wu pulls a sliver of wood from his cheek and with dry lips and salty palms, he peers out through the jagged hole. What he sees sends his blood plummeting into his boots. Hundreds and hundreds of Chinese troops. Soon they will be here and his school will be lost.

A red-hot poker stabs the ninja's chest. The boy in Japan, who had told everybody Wu had committed the murder, had been his elder brother. And now Tor had betrayed him too. Betrayed his new SWARM family just like his brother had betrayed his family.

Wu feels a fool. He thought Tor to be a

kindred spirit; like himself, forced to flee his country, to live a life on the run. The major will pay for this, he thinks angrily. Wherever he is, whatever he is, he will find a way to put the lying weasel in his coffin.

With the speed of a cheetah, he sprints from the Rimankya Room and up the corridor to the scullery. There, he pulls up the trapdoor to the cellar.

At the bottom is a tiny low-roofed office. A boy sits in it by a wall of levers, buttons and swirling cogs.

'SIR!' The boy hops to his feet and bows. 'Can I help?'

But Wu blasts him with a stony look and the boy's jaw snaps shut.

Grabbing up a pencil and a pad of paper, the ninja begins to scribble. Thirty seconds later, he rips off the top sheet and hands it to the boy. 'Here! Send this to SWARM HQ,' he commands him. 'Now!'

Using Morse code 'dot-dash-dot' the telegraph system allows letters to be sent all over the world. It is very modern, only a month or two old, and Wu is hoping Major Tor will not know it exists. Counting on him not knowing the words he has just written will now be whisked off to a tiny office in Vladivostok. From there they will fly down a cable to Berlin, Paris and finally to SWARM HQ deep under London.

Only a day or so from now, three weeks prior to Major Tor's arrival in London, Mr Spider will be handed a scrap of paper, on it the identical words Wu had just written a half a planet away in Hornet Temple.

Wu is just happy he did not tell the major what the cable under his window is really for.

The boy nods. Then, tentatively, he asks, 'Who's attacking us, Sir?'

'Government troops,' spits Wu bitterly. 'Major Tor betrayed us.' He shoots the boy a cold look, his eyes narrowing. 'Günter, yes, from Germany or...'

'Yes, Sir,' the boy interrupts him. 'Frankfurt.'

Gravely, Wu nods. 'Well, Günter of Frankfurt, when this message is wired, you can stay and fight or run. It's up to you.'

For a moment, Wu puts his hand on the boy's shoulder. Then he sprints over to a shadowy corner of the cellar. He rolls back a barrel of gunpowder to uncover a hole in the

floor.

'Remember,' he calls back to the boy, 'a ninja's duty is to flee in the face of insurmountable odds.'

Watching the ninja crawl down into the hole, he reminds Günter of a fox scurrying off to cower in his den. The man's a coward; and to think he actually looked up to him.

For the tiny blink of an eye, the boy is tempted to scarper too. But deep down he knows he cannot run. No matter what Wu says, honour is important to him. There's no way he can just run off and not help his fellow ninjas in battle.

Grudgingly, he begins to tap out the message and moments later, it is sent. Crumpling up the paper in his tiny fist, he drops it to the floor.

Suddenly, there is the stomp of boots and his eyes cut to the roof. Dust in the rafters showers his curls and cheeks and a spider in a trembling cobweb rolls up in a ball. Slowly, knowingly, he pulls his sword.

For a second or two, he thinks of his mother and how his baby brother, Tommy, loved to play 'peek a boo' with him.

He wonders if they will miss him.

Then, with a yell of terror-blemished fury, he storms up the steps.

~

A spotty boy with wobbly chins and a limp creeps timidly down the steps to Hornet Temple's cellar, his sword still blotched with the blood of the fellow ninja he just murdered.

His name is Jomo and he is Cixi's spy in Wu's ninja school.

The murdered boy is not the first of Jomo's victims. Months ago, he killed another; threw him in Wu's pond of golden dart frogs. The boy, a wily kid from New York, had suspected him of spying and had to be gotten rid of.

Thankfully, Jomo sees there is no nobody in the cellar. His shoulders flop and he lowers his sword. He may be a coward, but he's no fool. He knows the benevolent Empress Cixi, for all her godly ways, will not thank him for dying for her.

The boy strolls over to the telegraph machine, a crumpled ball of paper crunching under his boot. With the instincts of a fox in a hen hut, he drops to his knee, picks up the torn,

trampled-on paper, and with a dry mouth, he unfolds it. It is written in English but, thanks to his mother, it is not a problem.

To Mr Spider from Mr Wasp STOP Major Tor betrayed SWARM STOP He murdered Mr Bee STOP He did not murder Yixin STOP Hornet Temple destroyed by Empress Cixi's troops STOP The culprit will be in London ETA 3 weeks STOP He must be captured STOP I will follow shortly on the Goyo-Goyuku ETA 5 weeks STOP Important STOP You suspected correctly STOP He has the yellow eyes STOP There is the hamrammr in him END OF MESSAGE

Thoughtfully, he folds up the innocent-looking scrap of paper and slips it in his tunic pocket. When he had been a boy in Jilin in Northern China, his mother had told him firmly to study English.

'Power is in the mind,' she had told him sternly, 'not in the sword.'

Even now, seven years later, he remembers how much he had hated doing it, trapped in his father's study, his Uncle Go Ti droning on and on and on about 'i's before 'e's, capital letters and full stops.

But now, it seems, his mother's prophecy had been spot on.

General Li will undoubtedly want to see this, he thinks slyly, and so will Empress Cixi. Gluttony smoulders in his pupils. He will be rewarded for this: jewels, chests of silver; maybe the empress will even promote him.

'General Jomo,' he utters smugly. His mother will be over the moon.

Saturday, 27th March, 1872
20 Days to Assassination Day

0620 hours, London Docks

It is frigidly cold in London, the sort of damp windy day common to the island. Swollen clouds with drooping stomachs hover over the slowly waking city keen to wash away the morning fog and the stink rising up from the sewers and the murky waters of the Thames.

I hop off the deck of the Sweeper, a hundred and fifty foot clipper and my taxi all the way

from China, and with a cheery wave to the crew, I amble up the dock.

It's still very early, but the wharf is awash with pipe-smoking fishermen dropping off barrels of fish; mostly cod and the odd flapping salmon destined for Billingsgate fish market. The whalish hulls of cargo ships sit anchored to the dock too. Dockers called Lompers and Whippers, mostly bankrupt butchers and murderers on the run, carry barrels of rum and chests of coffee from the ships' holds to mammoth sheds constructed of rusty bolts and driftwood walls. There they will be counted and a tax put on them.

I stop for a moment to watch a boy cut the fins off a sturgeon and skin it. He then throws the flesh to a second boy who cuts it into strips and dips them in a bucket of salt.

I look to the ships moored not twenty feet away, a forest of masts and sleepy sails, but I cannot spot the Flying Spur. I had vaguely hoped she'd be in port and I'd be able to recover my rifle and box of inks, and catch up a little with the crew: tell them how, back in November, I'd been kidnapped and had not simply skulked away in the night.

But sadly, no joy.

Walking on, I spot at the very top of the dock what can only be a motor car. I remember I had seen a photo of Dr. Trevithick's famous Puffing Devil, the very first motor car, at a fayre in Paris. It had reminded me of a clumsy elephant.

But this is very, very different.

It is elegant, even stylish, from the spoked rubber wheels to the winged angel on the hood. The wood is glossy and the silver chrome has been buffed to mirrors. Her perfect silhouette is only slightly marred by the words 'Malum instet in timidi victima' etched on her front passenger door. My Latin is poor and I wonder what it says.

A stern-looking chauffeur sits stiff-backed on the driver's bench. He looks pretty old, his skin putting me in mind of a speckled duck egg. He has on a black tunic and a black cap - well, I think so anyway. With my present handicap, his uniform might just as well be banana-yellow.

I feel my fists curl up. Slumped on the hood in a flared polkerdot dress and resembling a bottom-heavy vase is Granny Moth, Gurli's

murderer. The volcano in me stirs, but I know now of a way to control my fury, in my grandmother's words, to show this demon in me who's boss. After six weeks on a ship, I just think of her Junzi flowers: bamboo, the plum, the orchid and the chrysanthemum; how they blossom in the snow. Calm yet strong in the face of adversity.

On my trip to London, I often pondered over this 'evil' in my skull. Is it really there or is it simply a fantasy; a wall I put up to protect myself from the truth: that I am the demon. The monster.

But if it is only me, how is it I can jump ponds and stop bullets? How is it I can see on a moonless night and smell terror in men from a hundred yards away? Yet, when I chew on a plum, it is just bitter and dry. And who is this demon who whispers to me, and who is the angel who so cleverly blankets his evil words?

My thoughts often return to the day Skufsi Tennur sunk his teeth into me. That day, I had changed. Is it possible, I wonder, that there is now wolf blood in me. But no, it cannot be. A child's story for stormy nights; the stuff of silly legends.

Whatever it is in me, this power, this need to hurt, even kill, I will channel it. For now it is my ally and it can help me to destroy SWARM. Then, when this is all over and Spider is tucked up in his coffin, I will find a way to destroy it.

So, with the Junzi flowers firmly set in my mind and the volcano firmly plugged, I march over to my enemy.

'Welcome, Mr Locust.' Nervously, she dabs a hanky to her top lip but I still spy her rotten teeth. They match perfectly the colour of the driver's cap and tunic. Well, probably! 'A fun trip, I hope.'

I can tell this is difficult for her. But then, I did destroy her plans for Norway and, undoubtedly, her boss, Spider, had not been a happy man. There's a fury in her, festering in her belly. I can almost smell it. I can smell it. The unmistakable stench of hatred. I know it well for it sits in my own stomach too.

'Very,' I reply curtly.

'Good. Good. No trunk, I see.'

'No. Just me and my trusty sword.' I tap the hilt suggestively.

'Hmm.' She licks her lips. 'Hop up then. I just hope the traffic is not too terrible.

DRIVER!' she yells. 'Keep off Oxford Street if you can and if a bobby stops you, just tell them who you work for.'

I eye her suspiciously. 'Where we off to, Moth?' Disrespectfully, I skip the 'Granny'.

A tiny sneer widens her nostrils. 'Major Tor, oops, silly me, Mr Locust, you must trust me. SWARM is your new family, and you and me,' she winks, 'well, we must be brother and sister now.'

She scowls at my scoffing tut. 'So be it,' she sniffs. 'If you must know, there is a room for you in the city, 27 Joy Street, very comfortable, just by the Queen's Club. It is important you sleep, for on Monday you will meet Mr Spider in SWARM HQ.' She eyes me keenly, her lips puckered up like a cat's bottom. 'And in the afternoon he will tell you everything you need to know for your first job.'

'Second job,' I correct her stonily. I hop up into the car, Moth on my heels.

'GO!' she hollers to the driver, 'AND STEP ON IT!' The door slams, the motor growls, there is a clunk and we trundle off.

The cabin is a metaphor for luxury with a velvety cloth roof and a snowy-white sheep's skin carpet so deep my boots almost drown in fluffy wool. There is even a bar in the corner. I spot a bottle of Champagne, Venue Clicquot, 1855. I remember General de Wimpffen had had the identical bottle in his tent in France.

'I can offer you Scotch or, perhaps, a Welsh port?'

I answer her with cold eyes and a cold shoulder, turning to look out of the window.

So in two days I will finally meet my archenemy, Spider. My hand rests expectantly on Tyrfing's hilt but I know I must not be in too much of a hurry to kill him. I'm the spy in the camp now. There is opportunity here to discover all of SWARM's little secrets and to destroy not only Spider, but every fly in his rotten web.

By now, Empress Cixi will know I did not murder Yixin and, undoubtedly, her troops have wiped out Hornet Temple. If Wu did not perish in the battle, he will have sent word of my betrayal.

I have three weeks.

Possibly four.

Then Spider will know of my plan and the element of surprise will be lost.

I remember Grandmother Toyi's words to me. How it is not my job to keep everybody in the world safe.

But, then, who will stop Spider and his assassins?

I know she thinks, months, years from now, I will feel sorry for what happened to Gripenstedt's son. I know she probably thinks my attempt to destroy SWARM will end only in sorrow. Well, maybe it will. But maybe that is the cost of stopping them and maybe it is I, only I, who can pay the bill.

But I will need help. A lot of help. Slowly, the corner of my lips twist up for I know just where to find it. Officer Jon Wayne of Scotland Yard. 'Hmm.' I wonder if he is still upset with me.

With interest I watch Piccadilly Circus rattle by, a toffee tin mix of butchers, aproned flower sellers and poky shops with windows full of umbrellas, flowery bonnets and shiny-buckled ankle boots. I spy a chimney sweep, a ladder hooked on his shoulder, then a muffin man, current buns balanced perfectly on a wooden platter hooked to his cap. Everywhere I see billboards for BOVRIL and DRINK

CADBURY'S COCOA, and I spot a poster for The Morgue Theatre, a play called Roped to a Corpse.

But it is the smells of the town that I enjoy the most. The butchers reek of old blood and rancid fat, the flowersellers of lavender and rose. I get a whiff of soot and porridge from the chimney sweep and from the muffin man, melted butter and warm ovens.

There is another smell too. It is the smell of the bakery. But it is not the freshly-baked rolls or the current buns filling my mouth with drool; it is the mice hidden in the walls. How I long to chew on them. I prefer them fresh, still kicking, the tiny tufts of fur tickling my tonsils. But in a stew will do, or in a piping hot curry.

The clipper I travelled to London on had been swarming with them and most days I cooked them for the crew. I told them it was swordfish and they happily swallowed my fib, and the honey-glazed rodents.

By my elbow, Moth natters on and on. If only she had an 'Off' lever. Thankfully, most of her dribbly gobbledygook is lost to the clatter of the wheels and the bellows of the butcher boys and flower girls on the street.

'LAMB! WELSH LAMB! PENNY A LEG!'
'DAFFODILS! HALF PENNY A BUNCH!'

But I do catch this, 'Yes! Yes! Tomorrow is very important. Our HQ is superb; very cleverly hidden too, impossible to find. But don't worry, I will show you where it is. And Mr Spider's wonderful to work for, if you don't upset him. Then he can be a little,' she titters hysterically, 'crabby.' Swallowing, she thunders on. 'You must be thrilled, Major, sorry, Locust, Mr Locust, your first, no, second job for SWARM. And what a job it is.'

My interest spiked, I turn to her. I can tell by the playful spark in her eye, she's dying to tell me. Oh well, if it will shut the old crow up. 'So, who must I murder?' I interrupt her. 'The Queen? The Bishop of Canterbury? Oh, I know.' I click my fingers. 'Your dentist. Now him I will shoot for free.'

But Granny Moth just titters, seemingly unruffled by my childish humour. 'William R Gladstone,' she tells me with a joyous hoot. She shoots me a scornful 'I dare you to' look. 'The Prime Minister of this cold, wet and very windy island.'

I think my eyes actually spin; I even drool a

little.

The car's wheels hit a rut with a bone-shaking 'CRUNCH!', perfectly matching the moment.

Then...

...it begins to rain.

2240 hours, 27 Joy Street, London

In my tiny room on Joy Street, I roll over and over on my bed, twisting and turning, clawing at my pillow.

I'm back in the crowded grotto of hooded men. I spy a golden throne and trot briskly over to it.

Still, they bow to me.

Still, it feels good.

I stop in front of the gilded stool. I see it is set with glimmering jewels; hundreds of them: diamonds, emeralds and a lone ruby the size of a man's fist. I want to sit on the stool, curl up on the toggled silk pillow, but is it not Skufsi Tennur's? If I do, will I not be insulting this wolf, this god they chant so ardently for?

The throne pulls on me, towing me in; it saps

on my will and in a moment of bold stupidity, I hop up on it. But, still, the men do not attack me. All they do is chant. 'Skufsi Tennur! Skufsi Tennur!' Louder now, louder and louder, on and on and...

I jolt up in my bed.

Suddenly, I get it. In my mind's eye, the men pull off their hoods and I look out over a swarm of yellow eyes. I'm Skufsi Tennur. I'm the god they chant for.

Follow Major Tor to London in

TOR
MUTINY'S CLAW

Printed in Great Britain
by Amazon